THE
AFTERLIFE
OF
STARS

JOSEPH KERTES

Little, Brown and Company

Copyright © 2014 by Joseph Kertes

Hachette Book Group supports the right to free expression and the value of copyright. The purpose of copyright is to encourage writers and artists to produce the creative works that enrich our culture.

The scanning, uploading, and distribution of this book without permission is a theft of the author's intellectual property. If you would like permission to use material from the book (other than for review purposes), please contact permissions@hbgusa.com. Thank you for your support of the author's rights.

Little, Brown and Company
Hachette Book Group
1290 Avenue of the Americas, New York, NY 10104
littlebrown.com

First U.S. Edition: January 2017
Originally published in Canada by Penguin Canada, September 2014

Little, Brown and Company is a division of Hachette Book Group, Inc. The Little, Brown name and logo are trademarks of Hachette Book Group, Inc.

The publisher is not responsible for websites (or their content) that are not owned by the publisher.

The Hachette Speakers Bureau provides a wide range of authors for speaking events. To find out more, go to hachettespeakersbureau.com or call (866) 376-6591.

Library of Congress Cataloging-in-Publication Data
Names: Kertes, Joseph, author.
Title: The afterlife of stars / Joseph Kertes.
Description: First U.S. Edition. | New York; Boston: Little, Brown and Company, 2017.
Identifiers: LCCN 2016016820 | ISBN 978-0-316-30811-3 (hardback)
Subjects: LCSH: Families—Fiction. | Family secrets—Fiction. | Domestic fiction. | BISAC: FICTION / Family Life. | FICTION / Jewish. | FICTION / Literary.
Classification: LCC PR9199.3.K4275 A38 2017 | DDC 813/.54—dc23
LC record available at https://lccn.loc.gov/2016016820

10 9 8 7 6 5 4 3 2 1

LSC-C

Book design by Marie Mundaca

Printed in the United States of America

Dedicated to the memory of Raoul Wallenberg
and Paul Hegedus
and to the memory of my parents, Hilda and Paul

Beware, O wanderer, the road is
walking too.

                    —*Rainer Maria Rilke*

THE AFTERLIFE OF STARS

ONE

ON OCTOBER 24, 1956, the day I turned 9.8, my grand-mother came to take me out of school in Budapest's sixth district. We were in the middle of reviewing decimal points because of a mistake a classmate named Mary had made. Other parents and grandparents were arriving too with the same aim, although no one had come yet to get Zoli, the boy who sat beside me.

My grandmother gripped my hand as we made our way down Andrassy Avenue. At the Oktogon, where many of the big avenues of the city met, a crowd had formed. We couldn't get by. A tank stood in the street, a bold red star shining on its flank. There were Russian soldiers too, but no one paid attention to them. Everyone was gazing up instead at eight Hungarian soldiers, one hanging from each lamppost around the Oktogon. My grandmother pulled hard on my arm, but not before I had joined the lookers.

Most of the Hungarian soldiers weren't dead yet. A couple had stuck out their tongues as they dangled—one seemed to be smiling, four others wriggled and bucked, but the nearest one to us, straight above my grandmother and me, looked down at us with evergreen eyes, but there was no anger in the eyes, or even light.

My grandmother breathed into the crown of my hair, sending hot tendrils down over me. "Come, please," she whispered, and I shuddered.

The crowd was quiet. Even the few people sobbing were doing it silently, swallowing the sound. From a little way down the street came the sound of an orchestra and a woman singing a sad song. I looked around until my grandmother turned me toward the music.

"It's a record," she said. "From over there."

We spotted an open window above a lacy café a half block away, the white tongue of a curtain flapping out from the window.

"It's Mozart," my grandmother said, steering me onward. "His 'Laudate Dominum,' I think. 'Praise the Lord,' it means. Why would anyone play that now?"

"Because they like it," I said.

"Yes, of course. Because they like it."

"Did you see the man's hair?" I turned back toward the Oktogon and the dangling men.

"Whose?" my grandmother asked me.

"The man with the green eyes."

I knew she had looked with me, but just for a second. The man's auburn hair was parted and brilliantined so that it shone even at this distance.

"Do you think he combed it for someone?" I asked.

"I don't know," my grandmother said. "His sweetheart, I suppose." I thought she might cry, but instead she said, "Now, please keep moving, my dear. We'll have cake. Let's have cake, at Gerbeaud."

"Now?"

"Yes, now. Let's have a treat. You can order anything you want. I know you want poppy-seed strudel."

She took me all the way to Vorosmarty Square. The cobblestones made me think of a great house lying on its side. From the top of the building opposite, two Russian soldiers, both sturdy women, unfurled a canvas sheet so big it covered a side of Kossuth's department store from roof to sidewalk. It was a vast portrait.

"Look, it's Papa Stalin," I said. I knew him right away from the picture above the clock in our classroom. He had the same smile and mustache, a mustache that was three times as impressive as Hitler's, which was little more than a black checkerboard square. I found myself smiling back at the giant face, like a circus face.

"Please," my grandmother said, giving my arm a tug. "The great father forgot himself," she said under her breath. "Forgot to leave. *Come,* Robert, please." And she pulled even harder on my arm now.

I was as excited about poppy-seed strudel as I was about Kaiser Laszlo, Gerbeaud's monkey in a golden cage. He squealed as soon as we walked in. I think he recognized me because I'd fed him some apple cake last time.

If I were the kaiser, I'd recognize everyone who fed me cake. He was wearing a bellman's blue cap and vest. He tilted his head in an appealing way and held out his little hairy hand.

At the table I felt warm, as if we'd come in out of a storm. The waiter placed our sweets and cocoas in front of us. My grandmother took out her compact and mother-of-pearl makeup case. I watched, dazzled, as like an artist she applied some lines and clouds, borders and dots. Once done, she fished out her monogrammed silver cigarette case, removed a cigarette from behind the garter, and tapped the end on the case before lighting it. I was just breaking off a corner of my strudel for the kaiser when the manager walked to the middle of the busy café, clapped her hands sharply, and called out to us, saying we all had to go. She was very sorry. The café was closing for the rest of the day, but we could take our cake with us. The waiters brought linen napkins in which to wrap up our things. For a moment I thought it was because they'd run out of cake, but the glass cases were full of colorful sweets. I noticed a colony of marzipan goblins and other figures. Our waiter brought me one of them, a marzipan monkey with a cap like the kaiser's.

A woman in a long mink coat brushed by us, trailing the scent of mothballs. For the longest time, I had thought that this was the scent of mink until my grandmother explained. The woman paused by the door to glance back at us but then peered down at her feet. She wore black patent leather shoes with very high heels and sharpened toes. They were pointed at something.

"Look," the shoes seemed to be saying. "Right there on the floor. Have a gander." Then, with their fine sense of direction, the shoes turned, aimed themselves toward the door, and took the woman out with them.

People were leaving quickly and abandoning their cake—most of them.

"What will happen to the kaiser?" I said. "They won't hang Laszlo, will they?"

"No, of course not. Not a thing will happen to him," my grandmother said. "He'll be here for us next time."

"When?"

"*Next* time," she said, as if she were saying "never."

We hurried home to find my parents rushing around the apartment and making telephone calls. My mother flitted from one room to the next. She smiled when she saw that I was home. "Sorry you had to leave school, my lambkin," she said, and then went about her business.

My brother, Attila, was already home. He was 13.7, and he had our mother's blond hair, while I had black hair, like our father's. Attila was also a head taller than I was, everyone kept pointing out. It made me want to plop an extra head on top of mine, a freaky one, possibly.

My brother was sitting on the sofa eating an apple. "We're leaving altogether, my lambkin," he said to me.

I sat down beside him. "Where are we going?"

He was chomping away but said, "West. We're going to the Wild West. You'll need your cowboy hat and spurs."

My brother wasn't saying any more. He acted as if he

knew but wasn't telling, so I said, "I saw the hanging men."

His face fell open. "What do you mean?"

"From the lampposts."

He turned his arctic blue gaze on me. "Which ones?"

I crossed my arms. "On Andrassy," I said. "At the Oktogon." I pictured the man with the green eyes and nicely combed hair, but I wanted to protect the secret of this man, so instead I said, "Some of the men had their tongues sticking out."

Attila jumped to his feet. "That is *not* what happened. You did not see hanging men, and they do not stick out their tongues. I know that for a fact."

I shrugged. "Ask Mamu."

Attila ran off to get our grandmother, and I could hear him yelling out questions at her. When he came back to me, he had whitened. His blue eyes looked like marbles dropped in snow. I thought he might want to strangle me. He glared, slapped at the arm of the sofa. "Are they still there?" he asked.

"What?"

"Are they still *hanging* there? *Shit.*"

He rushed out to the balcony and climbed onto the railing to peer out over the bronze head of Mor Jokai, the old Hungarian writer, whose statue sat at the top of our street, keeping watch over it. Attila turned toward me with his icy stare. Then he flew back past me to our bedroom, slamming the door behind him.

★   ★   ★

That night, as we got ready for bed, my brother looked inside his pajama bottoms—he did quite a study—then raised his arms, flexed, and faced the mirror, admiring the muscles and then the hairs sprouting from his armpits. "We are experiencing the balding of the world, my small brother." He tugged on a couple of the hairs. "These tufts are the last bits of hair left to us. But notice the apes are having none of it. They probably know something we don't."

"What?" I asked.

"I told you: it's something we don't know."

"How do you know it's anything, then?" I said.

Attila sighed but then moved on, which was his way. He peered down again into his pajama pants. "I would have made sperm a brighter color," he said, "if I had been the Lord God, Creator of the Universe."

"What color is it now?"

"You don't know?" he asked, smiling broadly. I shook my head. He said, "Do you want me to bring some forth for you to see?"

"No, I don't."

"It's a drab pearly cream color. It doesn't say how important it is, how exciting, how it makes babies, humans, soldiers, beauties, love, courage, heroism." The image of the hanging men shot through me, this time the ones with their tongues out. Attila was still talking. "These are children waiting to be born, or bits of children—the Beck bits, in our case—they're bits that carry messages, vital information about us, my golden hair, your black hair, my sparkling blue eyes, Mom's smile, our grand-

9

mother's niceness, our bravery—or at least *mine*." He slapped himself on the chest. "The color says nothing, or it says it is nothing. Blood is red. It makes declarations. It says alarm; it says *I am the living stream*. But sperm does not. It is dull and poorly designed, or at least poorly decorated. 'Give it something more,' I would have said to the Lord. 'Color isn't everything. Give the little sperms horns, or feathers.'"

"Feathers? Really?"

"Or full wings," he continued. "Just fly through air. Right now, the slithery bastards swim upstream. Why not give them wings? Give them noisemakers, or little voices, so that all together they could sound like a mob storming the gates."

Attila got into bed. I was still sitting on the edge of mine, waiting for more, I guess. I was staring at him, at the back of his golden head, his slender white neck. I was sure that even with a noose around his neck my brother would keep his tongue in his mouth, just to prove his point.

By the time I switched off the lights, he was asleep. He always fell asleep right away, even when our grandmother told us stories. Now I listened as she and our parents spoke in quiet but heated tones in the living room.

"We'll go to Nebraska or Utah," my father said. I didn't know those places. Now he turned on his loud-speaker voice. "Yes, we'll become Mormons. Lili, I want to become a Mormon, try on something new." He was creaking back and forth over the floor, and then he stopped. "We'll go to Canada. Why not

Canada?" I knew my father's cousin Adam lived in Canada.

"What are you talking about?" my mother asked. "And please keep your voice down."

My grandmother said we should go to Paris first to visit her sister, Hermina. It would be a good place to start.

"We'll *visit* Paris," my father said, too loudly. "We're not *staying* in Paris."

"Why don't we wait and see?" my mother asked.

"Because we've had enough of Europe," he said. "Have you not had enough of the old bitch?" He was blasting out his thoughts now. "The whole place should be paved over and turned into a parking lot."

"Simon, please," Mamu whispered. "This has been our home. It has always been our home. You would not have said this if your father were still around."

"He's not around. He is resting at last."

"Do you consider that a good thing?" his mother asked.

"It works for me."

"*Simon*," my mother said. "Why do you always have to go too far?"

"Here's what I know," my grandmother said, huffing. I imagined her getting to her feet. "I know that nobody knows anything. And some of us seem to know nothing with greater certainty than others."

No one answered. There was some shuffling of feet and some tinkling of glasses, but they went quiet soon after.

In the darkness, the bar of light that started at the foot of our door floated up like a wand into the ceiling. When the living room lights finally went out, I waded through the black milk of the night. I saw the green eyes of the hanging man up ahead in some forest, like the eyes of a woodland creature. I heard music—drumming—from the window and thought of Kaiser Laszlo, deprived all afternoon of his usual morsels. But it wasn't drumming. It was pounding. Our bedroom windows rattled in their casements and lit up as bombs fell in the distance, the sound muffled, as if I were listening through my pillow. I counted the seconds between the flashes and the sounds, the way Attila and I did with thunder and lightning, to see how far away it was. Then the hanging man's eyes drifted up again, greening over my sleep.

As Attila and I got dressed the next morning, it felt strange not to be going to school—like a holiday, but not a festive one. My father's cousin Andras and his wife, Judit, were over, and the whispering continued until Attila and I joined them. They were sitting in the kitchen having tea and walnut cake. Judit was as pregnant as could be and panted as she shifted this way and that, too small and slight to have all that baby stuffed inside her. She had a glow about her in the early morning lamplight and a constellation of copper freckles, which moved with her big smile.

She gave me a hug and kiss. Up close, she smelled of the sweet, powdery scent of a baby. "I hope I have a child as beautiful and smart as you boys," she said.

"You should be so lucky," Attila said, as he reached for a cup and panted extra hard, the way Judit was doing.

Judit wanted me to sit in her lap, but I said I was too big.

"You're not," she said.

"He is, my sweetie," my mother said, smiling.

But Judit had already pulled me down onto her lap and thrown her arms around me. Everyone was smiling then as things seemed to swirl around us.

"I just want a good child," Judit said. "A kind one."

"Oh, is *that* all?" my brother said. He had poured himself some espresso and was adding ten spoons of sugar.

"Yes," was the answer. Judit had a determined look in her eyes.

"Mamu and I saw people hanging our soldiers," I told her. "Russians."

Judit loosened her grip on me. "Oh, my dear Lord," she said. "Oh, dear dear Lord. My poor young Robert." She held my face by the temples, looked me in the eyes, then held my whole head too tightly.

There was a pounding at the door, quite a commanding one, and we all turned in that direction, as if to understand what it meant. We followed my father into the vestibule and huddled behind him, except for my brother, who stood by his side. It was Attila who opened the door. A man, a soldier the size of a tree, stood outside. He had such an overgrowth of beard that he could have supplied a whole room of teenagers with all the tufts they needed. He barked something at us in Russian.

The red star gleamed from his furry officer's cap. He

barked something again, and Judit squeaked and held her stomach.

The tree man paused, but then he entered the vestibule, parted us, and stepped up to Judit. He stared at her, gazed down at her belly, then bent down to listen there. No one knew what to do. He pointed a long finger at her stomach. Andras was ready to lunge at the Russian, and so was my brother behind him. Judit whimpered.

The man laughed as he straightened all the way up again. His mouth was like a jewel box, full of gold and glitter. He pushed past us and marched straight to our clock on the sideboard in the front room as if he knew right where it was. We followed him, and he waited for us to gather. He pointed to the clock, circled his long brown finger a number of times past the 12, and motioned that we were all to leave. Then, to our relief, he marched out again and slammed the door.

"We have until three o'clock," our father said to us. "And then we have to be gone."

"For how long?" I asked him.

"We don't know," my grandmother said gently.

"For about two centuries," Attila said, "before we check back in with them."

"What do you mean?" I asked.

"They want us to get out," Andras said. "Not out of the country." We weren't supposed to leave the country, weren't *allowed* to, actually. We were just supposed to find lodgings elsewhere.

"But we're not doing that," Attila said.

"Be quiet," our father said.

"We can't leave now," Judit said in a whisper. I could hardly hear her.

"We have to," her husband said. "Now is our only chance." The Hungarian rebels were rising up, he explained. There were breaks in the border. It would be the only time.

"But Andras," our grandmother said, putting her arm around Judit.

My brother looked straight at me. "We're leaving," he insisted. "Forever. I told you—we're going west."

"Why can't we just get the Russians to like us instead?" I asked.

Attila shook his head. "Lambkin, you're not too bright."

But my remark made Judit tear up. She embraced me and kissed me on the head before leaving with Andras.

The Russian was back within an hour, and he had brought other soldiers with him, two women and one man. But the original one with the beard was obviously overseeing the proceedings. They worked their way through our home more like movers than invaders. They acted as if we weren't there. From the china cabinet, they carefully pulled out Herend porcelain cups, saucers and platters, and a silver sugar box and teapot, wrapping them in cloth before placing them in large canvas sacks. Attila and I watched from the sofa.

They took down the paintings one at a time, leaving rectangular blond ghosts on the gold wallpaper. The largest of these was called *Christmas 1903*. It depicted two women dressed in dark coats and fur hats, one bent over a walnut secretary desk, writing a letter, the other looking out and down at us. Between them stood a potted Christmas tree on a table, festooned with bright ribbons and baubles and a star at the top. I always wondered why such a cheerful tree did not manage to spread its joy to the dark women in the parlor, who had most likely decorated it. Now the women were gone, together with their tree.

One solitary picture still hung on the wall among the ghostly rectangles. It was a drawing done by my brother of a Spitfire fighter plane tearing through the skies, spitting impressive bursts of fire. In the corner of the picture was the sun, and it too fired off spikes instead of rays of light. It was a sketch Attila had done in school, and our mother had had it framed in gold and hung over the gilded clock, in the shape of a double-headed eagle on the sideboard, which stood guard over the room. The fierce-looking bird was the emblem of the Austro-Hungarian Empire.

I had done a picture I knew my mother would like too, a watercolor of a weeping willow, but it was still at school. My teacher, Mrs. Molnar, had hung it up where the photographs of Stalin and Khrushchev hung, but on the opposite side of the classroom's wall clock. My tree was surrounded by other trees that also wanted to weep. I had given them their own tears in many colors flying off the leaves. My classmate David thought the other trees might have been sweating after a run, but I explained my intent. A year before, I had done another picture, in crayon, of sunflowers. It wasn't a field of sunflowers, exactly, but sunflower after sunflower, quite a few of them. My brother seemed to admire the picture. He said my flowers looked like the handiwork of God as a child, trying out designs for the sun. That wasn't my intent either. I didn't know where that picture got to, exactly.

One of the Russian women carrying a canvas bag looked at the Spitfire twice as she passed by us. We watched her closely. She removed her snug army cap to reveal straw-colored hair tied back tightly, giving her head the look of an onion. She paused by the drawing but walked on. The eagle watched with its four sharp eyes. On her third trip by, she picked up the eagle clock with a strong arm and wrapped it up like a mummy before bending over to make room for it in her heavy sack.

Attila studied the operation, kept glancing up at his own drawing in its precious frame, waited for her to leave our home with the sacks, and then tore off madly to our room.

I tiptoed to the dining room to see if the Russians had taken our bowl of rose cream chocolates. I cared less about the red crystal bowl than about the chocolates themselves. They were still there. I wondered if it would be all right to sit at the table and steal one. I took a chance. I peeled off the red foil wrapper and put the chocolate into my mouth whole, let its creamy sweet heart enjoy its new home. I didn't want to chew, to take a single bite. I laid my cheek against the cool surface of the dining-room table. My grandmother had bought this table for my parents for their "wood" anniversary, she told me. She said it was made of walnut by Sebastyan

Balaban, the famous furniture maker. He had told her it would last a thousand years. We had had it for eleven, just 1.1 percent of its life span, meaning some nice Russian family could enjoy meals and chocolates off it for 989 more years. I took another chocolate to eat in my room and one for my brother.

But I had a second table to visit first. It was the round-topped pedestal table in the front room. It was the one I always hid under when I was very young. Made of heavy black maple and standing on beastly wooden lions' paws, it sat between two dainty ladies' lamps in all its manly glory. I ducked underneath. I wanted to sit in its darkness for what might be the last time. When I was younger, I thought that this unlucky lion had grown a tabletop instead of a head, but when my brother taught me the facts of life, I realized that a lion and a table had lain down together to make this child. I hoped it was the table that was the mother. I ran my fingers through the carved fur and the hard claws and said my good-byes.

Something fell in the kitchen, but not a dish, because it didn't shatter. I jumped out and ran back to our room. My brother was holding his june bug collection up to the light of the window, but then he shelved it again. The collection had won him a science prize a couple of years back.

After that, things moved quickly. Our father told us we could each take what we could carry, no more. I snuck out again to the front room, peered in, making sure there was not a single Russian in the room. Then I ran to the sideboard, no longer watched over by the two-headed eagle, and removed a golden cup and saucer. They looked as if they might have come from an old palace, but they were small, like children's dishes. My parents drank espresso out of them when we had company. I hid them in my shirt and slunk away toward the bedroom. I dashed out again, one last time, snatched Attila's Spitfire drawing off the wall, opened my shirt, slipped it past the buttons, and slid it all the way to the back above my belt before buttoning up my shirt again.

I ran into the Russian soldier in the hall and thought I'd been caught. My face burned. Instead of stripping me of my booty, he handed me a Russian nesting doll—*matryoshka,* he called it—and I bowed, feeling the corners of the picture frame claw my skin, before retreating to my room. I slipped the picture under my bed. The brightly painted *matryoshka* doll came apart, and a series of smaller dolls lived inside, all the way down to a puny one. She was a colorful wooden bean, little more.

As I admired them, Attila said that I was a girl. I countered with my cowboy hat, spurs, cap gun, and holster, all of which I placed in my satchel with the reassembled *matryoshka*. With my back to Attila, I rolled my cup and saucer each into its own sock, pulled his drawing out from under the bed, and finally added my marzipan monkey, still blanketed in the linen cloth from Gerbeaud. The cloth had a *G* monogram.

"Come with me, my one true love," Attila said behind me. "I want to show you something, over by Heroes' Square. I hear something is happening there."

"Where the big Stalin is? The statue?"

"Just come," he said.

"Shouldn't we tell somebody we're going?"

"Not if we want to get out of here. We'll be back before anyone notices; don't worry."

Of course we wouldn't be, but I knew better than to argue. From the hard look on my brother's face, I had a hunch he was taking me to where there were twice as many hanging men as I had seen and that his hanging men would be Russians, not Hungarians.

We slipped by the commotion in the kitchen, and Attila led me on a trot through the confused streets of our city, streets full of people not going about their business as they usually did, but acting alarmed, whispering rather than talking to one another. Nobody looked tired or bored, as they did on other days.

Attila had me by the hand. Everyone was pulling hard on my arm these days. We were rushing down Andrassy Avenue, the same way I'd come with my grandmother, when a tall woman came out of a white building, a woman with long, straight black hair, wearing a black hat as wide as an umbrella and a black satin cloak, which flowed and fluttered with each strong step she took. She was heading straight toward us. My brother wanted to pick up the pace, but I slowed us down. I was staring.

"What do you want with her?" my brother asked.

The woman had black eyes, black eye shadow. I had stopped altogether now.

"Do you want to take her home with you? She's a black limousine, rearing up on her hind wheels."

20

She saw us, saw Attila and me gawking, and glared at us before crossing the street, though she could easily have run us over.

When we turned a corner, we just about ran down a man ourselves, a beggar holding out his hand. Attila stopped. He seemed to be out of breath for some reason. The man was a Gypsy, one-legged, one-armed, propped up against a bakery whose window had been shattered. In the window, a single dingy lace curtain clung to its rod, shaking its head no in the breeze. A loaf of bread sat inside on the counter, along with a cake that looked blue in the light.

The poor man stood out of the wind on his only leg and held out his only hand. He was like a badly designed tree, with a single branch held out to catch rain.

"What about today?" the man said to us.

"Today?" Attila asked.

"Yes," the Gypsy said.

"I don't know," my brother said.

A crutch lay behind the man, together with a battered violin. "Are you back now?" he asked, his hand still held out to us.

My brother looked at me. I expected him to say, "Let's go," but instead he wanted to stay.

I found a single coin in my pocket, put my hand around it. I stepped up and said, "Yes, we've been away, but now we're back. Have you been waiting for us?"

"Oh, a young girl," the man said. Attila grinned broadly. "I have been waiting," the man said. "Lucky girl."

My voice hadn't broken yet was the problem, and if it

didn't soon, I was going to take a rock to it. Compared to me, my brother sounded like a grown man, a man of the world.

I looked into the milk of the man's blue eyes and realized he couldn't see. "How do you play that violin?" I asked. "How do you manage?" I picked it up for him. It still had its shapely *f* holes, but it was battered—an *I* and an *O* plus some punctuation marks had punched their way through too.

"I haven't played for years," the man said. "The old girl is like a pet I don't have to feed much," he said, laughing. "Are you two musicians?" We didn't answer. "No, of course you're not," he said. "You're someone I stopped on the way to something. That's what I do, stop people on their way to something else."

A young woman flew by us, the whites of her eyes blazing. She turned down an alley between two tall gray stone buildings. She scared me. I had thought she was coming right at us. It was impossible to tell whether people were running to something or from something.

"Actually, I am a musician," my brother said. He was grinning again.

The man lowered his begging hand and said, "What do you play?"

"I play piano," he said, "and my sister sings."

"Do you?" the man said, genuinely pleased.

I pulled on Attila's arm now. I felt we should give the man a coin and go.

"What sorts of things do you sing and play?" the Gypsy said.

22

"We can do 'Pur ti miro' by Claudio Monteverdi," my brother said.

"Ah, the duet."

The man began to hum, and though I had never heard it myself, I said, "Yes, that's it."

"Can you do anything by Bizet? Can you perform some songs from *Carmen*?"

"Yes, my sister can, some of them."

"Can you sing 'Habanera'?"

I wanted to tear Attila to pieces. I felt my breakfast coming up.

The man started to sing himself, with a sad, raspy voice. If he had not been blind, I'm sure he would have closed his eyes. Now my brother wanted to leave, but I stood firm. I felt suddenly warmed by the song, warmed by the poor man. My grandmother had played the record a hundred times. I started singing along with the man, every word, without knowing what the French words meant.

L'amour est un oiseau rebelle
Que nul ne peut apprivoiser,
Et c'est bien en vain qu'on l'appelle,
S'il lui convient de refuser. . . .
L'amour! L'amour! L'amour! L'amour!

I stared into the man's face. I was sure I could see the thoughts moving behind his eyes like bits of glass.

He said, "You have nice tone, young lady."

"She does," Attila said. "That was nice," he said to me, and I think he meant it.

"Now, listen," the man said. I was still holding his violin, and he pushed it up against me. How did he even know I'd been holding it? "It's magic: listen."

I put my ear against one of the extra holes in the instrument's belly, as if it were a seashell.

"Can you hear that?" I heard nothing. "Can you hear the song?"

I could hear a wet wind now and was sure I could hear the river. "What kind of wood is it made of?" I asked.

"Violin wood," he said. "From the violin tree."

I offered it to Attila to try, but he declined. He wanted to go. I set down the violin where it had been. The torn awning flapped above our heads. I reached for the Gypsy's hand to give him my coin, and his hand closed greedily on mine.

"We have to go," I said.

He brought my hand up close to his lips. "I hope you have a very good reason for coming back, young lady," he said to the hand before letting it go.

I glanced at it to see if it had been soiled. I wanted to wipe it on something. "I do," I said.

"Yes," my brother said.

Another cold breeze blew up, and I shuddered.

The man still aimed his blind gaze at us. "It must be good," he said. "You must have a very good reason. Life and death."

Attila turned away from the man, suddenly panicked. He gave me a painful yank this time, and we took off toward Heroes' Square.

I felt a little strange, but I could hardly wait to see

the square again. It had been some time since I'd been there. I had come with my class on a clear day last spring. Stalin had stood like a Titan in the square on a high stone pedestal, a bronze man more impressive than a building. (If you want to make someone look like the Lord himself, my advice would be to make him big, his right arm raised high, his hand upturned, focusing the blue lens of heaven.)

When Attila and I turned the corner from Andrassy Avenue onto Dozsa Way, at first I thought we'd come to the wrong square. Perched on Stalin's pedestal were two boots the size of boilers, but no Papa.

"There!" Attila said, clapping his hands and hooting. We ran like mad toward the pedestal. Attila hooted again and jumped.

Stalin lay toppled behind his high stone platform. He was entangled in ropes and chains, like a colossus hoisted from the sea. But his big bronze boots still stood. Rope ladders hung from them.

There were surprisingly few people in the square. They covered their open mouths when they saw what we saw and hurried away, as if the fallen god's dark angels were still hovering, about to take revenge.

But Attila was fearless. He pulled me along like a dog toward the fallen father.

There was a shot, dinging something. I checked the windows all around the square, the trees, the moving shadows. Another shot pocked the pedestal.

My brother's tone sharpened. "Come!" he said. "Hurry." He was several rungs up one of the rope ladders. "Come!" he barked again.

I followed him. We scrambled up the sagging ladders. Who could have invented such a thing? I banged my elbow on the stone, scraped the knuckles of my left hand.

Attila was already on top. Several Russian soldiers came running toward their bronze leader from the other side.

Attila helped me reach the top of the pedestal. "We have to get inside."

"Inside *what?*"

"The boots. One each. There's a ladder up the far side of that one. You take that. I can get up this ladder."

"We're going inside the *boots?*"

Attila was hoisting himself up the ladder, moving his hands and feet like a monkey.

I clambered up the second ladder. "What are we doing?" I grunted.

"We'll be like Mother Goose. We'll be the Brothers Goose."

Attila waited for me. Once I made it to the lip of the boot, I was surprised to see how cavernous it was inside, taller than I was and much darker than the bright day. My brother gestured to me to raise the rope ladder—pull it up with all my might—and let it fall inside the boot. I watched him do it first with his ladder, then I did mine. The ladder was bony and heavy. I didn't think to use it once I had dropped it in and instead slithered down into the boot. I took quite a spill, landing on my shoulder at the bottom. I'd heard my brother sensibly drop feetfirst into his boot.

What now? I was quaking, my teeth clacking. I looked

up into Stalin's blue heaven. I was overcome with dread that we would soon become the Brothers Corpse and that it would have been a more glorious death to be strung up in the Oktogon. If we were to come out of this alive, my father would beat us, as he must. The inside of the boot darkened for a moment, and I thought what a good idea clouds were. I wondered what paintings of the sky would look like without them. We'd have to use a very rich blue without them, very pure, and without any brushstrokes showing. And what about rain? My brother always questioned whether things had been created or had evolved.

"It is interesting to think about things evolving," he once told me. "But it's more dazzling to think of them as being created." He said, "People want there to be a God. They need it."

"Why?" I asked.

"Because you can't pray to evolution."

For me, at the time, the difference was only a matter of gradual versus sudden. Though I struggled with such things, I was less concerned about them than interested in just the fact of them. What, I wondered, must it have been like to be the first person to experience rain? *What are these? There's a heavenly river, and it is breaking up. These are pieces of river. Pieces of lake. What is going on? Am I going to shrink or expand or drink or drown?*

A shot clanged against my boot or Attila's. My teeth clattered like mad, like something loose inside me, a box of buttons.

Then, just as suddenly, a calm settled over me like a gossamer net. Was this the end? Would they find us in these boots? Would Attila jump out like the warrior rebel he was and take the bullet he was born to take? Would the Hungarians come to finish Stalin and complete their triumph? Would the Russians come first and fill the boots with concrete instead, monuments to Stalin, the Ever Standing? If they found my brother and me, would they make examples of us, chain us to the boots until the vultures came to peck out our eyes? Was there honor in that?

The soldier of the Oktogon dangled before my eyes like a clear statement, and I knew that Attila and I would not die like legends but like jokes, the Brothers Grimm without a tale, our family shaking their heads, not allowing our names to be uttered again.

Attila was quiet in his boot. I wanted to call out to him but felt it best not to. I edged my way into the dark front of the boot, where Stalin's toes would have been, and then Attila loudly whispered my name. I crawled away from the toe, and he was there at the top of my boot. He must have pulled himself up.

"Let's go, my tender love," he said. "It's all clear."

"How do you know?"

"Look at me. I'm not being shot at." He climbed down into my boot and lifted me onto the rope ladder, pushing me up before climbing out himself.

We flew down Damjanich Street and almost ran into a tank clattering to the right of us. These beasts bruising around the streets were less like vehicles and more like instant buildings plopped down in the middle of the street, daring you to pass.

A squad of young men and a single young woman, a brunette with a determined look on her pretty red face, turned a corner and came toward us. They were chanting, *"Szabadsag! Szabadsag!"*—Liberty! Liberty! and waving a Hungarian flag with its familiar bars of red, white, and green, but with the Communist insignia at its center cut out, leaving a hole.

More shots were fired from somewhere, clipping the stone face of a nearby building. The squad of young people scattered. My brother grabbed me by the shoulder and yanked me into a doorway guarded by two stone lions. They stood on their hind legs, holding up the entrance, seeming to hold up the whole building. Sometimes it was angels who watched over an entrance, sometimes shapely stone maidens. But these were lions. It must have been a very heavy building. Stone lions will do things for you that real ones won't.

We waited several minutes, waited for quiet, before tiptoeing out and veering swiftly to the left until we got to Rakoczi Street. I could not catch my breath— I didn't even want to try. I could breathe later, I told myself.

Up ahead, a man stood calmly outside the Urania movie theater. He was dressed in a brown gabardine suit and wore a matching brown fedora. He was lighting a cigarette, turning away from the wind that brought us. The Urania was white and had Moorish windows. It always beckoned like a foreign land, like an exotic Arabian bazaar laden with wild and exquisite gifts, gifts with horns and warm gems.

We caught up to the man just as he exhaled his first full puff of smoke, and a shot sounded, taking off his hat. For a stark and childish moment, I tried, in my own mind, to trace the path of the bullet through the man's head as it knocked over everything in its path: his day, his night, his next puff of smoke, his dinner plate of veal *paprikas,* his smiling daughter holding up a glass to the light to see if it was cracked, his wife entering the dining room with the wine, wiping a damp hand on her apron.

The bullet might as well have struck us too, my brother and me.

"Let's go!" Attila snapped. He pulled me straight through the doors of the Urania, the white doors splattered now with blood.

An unsuspecting young woman, no bigger than a fawn, sat in her ticket booth. She smiled at us.

I was gasping, panting. "A man has been shot," I said.

"A man?" She rose with a creak from her chair to look out, raised her hand to her heart. "Oh," she said. The hand went to her mouth. She started to cry, sobbing, then hiccuping.

"This way," Attila said.

"What?" she said. She was still looking outside, probably at the blood on the glass.

"Now!" snapped my brother. "Now," he repeated, more gently. He was pointing into the theater, the promised darkness.

My teeth were clattering again. The fawn girl's white

skin had turned blotchy with fright, her eyes wide and a crazed white. She pattered to the front of the theater near the screen and straight out a side door. I thought we were going to follow, but my brother pulled me down low into the seat beside him.

There, in the darkness, Tarzan unleashed a sound like a jungle aria. The Urania was showing *Tarzan the Ape Man*. The theater was majestic, with its tall Arabian arches. A young couple sitting in a private box above us ignored Tarzan and Jane. They were making a meal out of each other's ears and lips. Would their love shrink when they found the fallen man outside? Would Tarzan have stopped to help the man in the brown suit?

Attila stared at the screen.

So we were going to sit now and watch a movie? We had just seen a real man's head explode, but now we'd watch *Tarzan the Ape Man*? There was an absoluteness to events as Attila lived them. It is sleep time, and now I will sleep. It is eating time, and now I will eat. It is ducking-into-a-theater time, and now I will duck. Once in the theater, I will watch a movie, which is what we do in a theater.

I could not draw one deep breath. Tarzan fought a lion. Jane was pretty. Tarzan swam with crocodiles. Jane loved Tarzan. Tarzan trumpeted through the jungle. Cheetah cringed. But where was Kaiser Laszlo? Where was the man in the brown hat? Who would carry him away? What time was it? Had the Russians expelled our parents? Did our parents think we were dead?

"I'm going," I said and got to my feet. Attila couldn't

take his eyes off the screen. "I'm *going*," I said again, and marched toward the front of the theater, where the fawn had disappeared.

Attila slapped at the armrest but followed. I took a last look up at the solitary couple in the box, but they had no interest in the world beyond their faces. Attila heaved open the side door with his bum. The sun's yellow smack blinded us, but we ran through it toward home as a cool wind blew up from the Danube, flecked with dust and leaves. Soon enough we could make out the familiar landmarks of our neighborhood and let down our guard a little. It was not until then that I finally found the meat of the air and gulped it.

I stopped for a moment. "Why did they shoot the man with the brown hat?" I said.

"I don't know," my brother said. He took my hand.

"What was the man doing?" I asked.

"He was lighting a smoke."

"And he got shot for that?"

I stopped, but Attila pulled us along. "Not for that," he said. "For stopping where he did, for being a standing target. For sport."

We got home just ahead of the Russians, who were late. When we slipped through the door, we were met by our father. I'd never seen him in such a fury. He was a snorting bull. He lifted Attila by the collar of his shirt, a mighty act, since my brother was almost full grown.

"You Russian!" Attila shouted at him.

Our father banged Attila up against the wall. But the matadors swooped down on them: Andras, Judit, our mother and grandmother. My father let Attila down but raised his fist like a biblical figure at both of us.

"Don't hit them!" Judit said. She embraced her swollen stomach, gasping and looking as if she might faint. "Oh," she said to her belly. She staggered back into the living room with the help of her husband.

But our mother had already slipped between our father's raised fist and my brother's golden head. Our mother hugged and kissed my brother and me strenuously, squeezing too hard. "My lambs, my lambkins," she said.

Our grandmother stood behind her, the disappointment on her face equal to my father's fury, as if her faith in life had been shaken, her faith in love. Just as she hugged me hard too, Attila broke free, bellowed like Tarzan, pounded his chest, and flew off to our room. I lost my breath again. My heart took off without a runner. The dead man in brown rose up in front of me.

My father snorted and slapped at his sides. "We have to go."

"Simon," my mother said through her tears. "We have our sons back."

"Yes," he said. "And we have to go. Now!"

We went to get our few things. When we returned to the vestibule, we could hear Judit in the living room with Andras. "The Russians are distracted just now," Andras was saying, "but not for long. They'll send in reinforcements, and when they do, we'll be stuck here. Our baby will be born here and grow up here."

"Is that so bad?" Judit whispered. "We grew up here."

"It will be bad, worse than we have known."

A short while later, Andras and Judit joined us in the hall. We were all leaving together, Andras and Judit included. They had brought their bags to our apartment, including Andras's dentist's case, as well as a rolled-up carpet, a very old Persian one featuring a bird of paradise, which they treasured. My father pulled his leather satchel, which contained his tool-and-die instruments, onto his shoulder.

Minutes later, the Russians came, not a friendly group like the first one, and they pointed the way outward, out of our home.

TWO

MY FATHER HAD ARRANGED for a small Hungarian army truck to take us to the Keleti railway station. The truck was waiting for us at the corner of our street, where the statue of Mor Jokai gazed out at Andrassy Avenue. Judit and Andras climbed into the back. Andras asked Attila and me what had taken us so long.

"We went to look at something," Attila said right away.

"Come, get in," Judit said. "Come, boys." She was patting the bench seat on either side of her. She looked shiny red and bursting. A couple of Hungarian soldiers helped us load our belongings into the back.

It was not far to the station. People were cheering and chanting. A tank with the familiar red Russian star sat dead but still fuming in front of the station. Teenagers danced around the steel beast, waving the flags of Hungary with the holes cut out of the center. "Out, tyrants," they were singing, and chanting. "Freedom, freedom, freedom."

Behind them rose the Keleti station, as great and grand a palace as any ever made. Here, the train emperors and empresses rolled in and out, in and out, welcomed by the great glass eyes and arms of the building. A stone angel sat at its crown, flanked by attendants and steeds, blessing the path.

But when we stepped inside, the imperial trains were already choked with people. There was such a frenzy in the station that it seemed as if everybody wanted to take flight, but we were all pinned down by gravity, penned in by the way-high roof and rafters. I looked around for some of my classmates. It would have been nice to see Mary now, just to know she was heading out too, her notes about decimal points stashed in her bag. I couldn't see anyone I knew. A man walked by us with a small table upside down on his head. Its legs were smooth and curved like a lady's. We pushed in, and I found someone my age. He was gripping a dog—too tightly, I thought—a terrier, who looked at me with furry eyes. I wanted to pet the dog, but he was having none of it— nor was his owner, who moved away.

"Sold out," we started to hear. "Sold out for today and tomorrow. No seats. Sold out."

The last of the ticket windows was closing. A single uniformed attendant weaved through the crowd, telling people they could spend the night on the cots around the sides of the building, where the soldiers used to sleep. "Find yourself a cot," he was telling people, "or please return home."

Beside us, Judit groaned.

"Can you not find two seats on the train?" our mother asked the attendant, gesturing toward Judit and Andras. "Just for them?" She smiled her radiant smile.

"Please," Andras said to the man.

"I have no seats," the man said. "I don't even have standing room." He hurried away.

My father had on a look like someone overcooked, ready to burst into flame. "We need tickets!" he shouted to no one in particular. The attendant hurried away from us. "Tickets! I'll pay double for tickets!"

"Simon!" our mother said to him.

"We'll be stuck in this place forever."

"I have gold," Andras said. "Let's offer a ring, earrings."

My grandmother put an arm around my brother's shoulders, mine too, but Attila slipped free.

"I can get us tickets," he said. "Give me the cash and jewels."

Andras looked at my father. He seemed to be awaiting some kind of instruction, but then a woman approached us. She was wearing an apron embroidered with folk colors, but she also wore a brooch pinned to her sweater just below the shoulder, a big gold brooch in the shape of Hungary, with jewels where the cities were and a snaking blue line meant to be the Danube. Her two front teeth were gold too.

"I have tickets," she said to us. "How many do you need?"

"How is that possible?" our mother said.

"Seven," our father said. "How much do you want for them?"

"I want the gold ring and earrings," she said, glancing at Andras, "but I want more."

My father was shaking. I thought he was going to hit the woman—punch her in the gut, possibly, and rob her. "What else?" he said through the cut of his teeth.

"I want your address and the key to your house."

"No," our mother said.

"One Jokai Street, second floor," our father said, standing very close to her, the brooch of Hungary bending between them. He found the key in his pocket and held it up high in the air.

"There are Russians in our house," our mother tried.

Our father glared at her.

The woman counted out seven tickets. She appeared to have as many left over. "The ring, the earrings, and the key," she said.

Our father snatched the tickets from her and handed over the key while Judit removed her ring and earrings.

Even waiting to depart on board the westbound train, we thought we would be stopped. Attila said he was ready if we were. Everyone looked around expectantly, but no Russians came.

The train was to leave in two hours, but it was easily three before it did.

At last, we rolled out into the evening. There weren't enough seats, and there was hardly enough standing room. My grandmother held my hand as we stood in the corridor and jiggled along, my satchel clamped between my feet. Attila helped our grandmother with her bag. He asked if she was taking a boulder to Utah or Canada, and a man nearby told us that during the war there was a building called Kanada in a camp at Auschwitz. Kanada was where all the valuables, like gold jewelry and gems, were stored. I wondered whether *Christmas 1903* was headed there.

Attila poked me in the back. He spoke right into my ear so the others wouldn't hear. He made me promise that if I were the first one to be strung up in the Wild West, I would stick out my tongue for him.

Then someone clasped me around my knees, and I saw a little girl in a frilly pink dress standing there. Behind her, crawling on all fours, was her baby brother, and behind them both was their red-faced mother. I looked down and asked the girl how old she was.

"I'm three," she said.

"And what about your baby brother?"

"Oh, he doesn't have a number yet," she said, very serious, and I tried not to laugh or even smile.

The three of them pushed on toward the toilets.

The train lurched, and Judit gasped and held the side of her stomach. Andras embraced her. He had his dentist's case with him, and some clothing and bedding in another sack. My father was carrying Andras and Judit's rolled-up Persian rug along with his tool bag.

The countryside outside our window was dark now. Only a single bomb lit up the glass, but I could not hear its pop.

Before long, the train squealed to a halt, but not at a station, just somewhere between stops, a place surrounded by fields. The conductor told us all to get off, and we helped Judit and my grandmother down before we started walking, the whole mob of us heading off in the same direction. The scent of night was heavy around us.

We left the railroad tracks behind and walked mightily toward the border, hundreds of us, many hundreds, like thieves through the dark. Now and then a bomb fell, and each time it did, Attila and I looked up to see who was dropping them. If they were celestial creatures, they flew without lights. They flew like bats. Judit whimpered and then yelped as if she were walking barefoot. My grandmother was beside me on my right, Attila on my left, and our parents were up ahead, keeping pace with Andras and Judit, our mother supporting Judit.

The sun had deputized the moon to give us light. Still, it was very dark—the stars were not much help—until a bomb went off again, again from nowhere. Something struck my brother, and he fell against me. My grandmother and I stopped and crouched beside him on the cool ground. My grandmother fumbled through her bag until she found her lighter. Its flame was as bright as a knife blade. It shone on a man's shoe. The top of the shoe was red and steaming. My brother had been struck by a man's shoe with the foot still inside it. Some of the blood dripped down his neck.

He jumped to his feet. "Where are these damn bombs falling from?" he said. He was rubbing at the side of his face where the boot had struck.

"They're not falling," our grandmother said. "This is a minefield we're crossing."

"Oh," my brother said, and then he took off like a bird.

"I should lift you up," my grandmother said to me. "It's not far now."

"You can't. I'm too big. I should be lifting you up."

She clenched my hand, our feet alive to every step as we walked.

It struck me just then how very keen I was on lamplight, its quiet little yellow show, and how nice it would be to have some in the field.

"Oh," I said, and I stopped.

"What's the matter?" my grandmother asked. She began searching for her lighter again but couldn't find it this time.

"My teacher, Mrs. Molnar, will be very upset with me," I said. "We have to tell her when we're going to be absent. We didn't tell her anything."

"Mrs. Molnar will understand this time."

"A boy in my class named Zoli was once strapped when he didn't say."

"This time is an exception, Robert. Mrs. Molnar herself is probably not far behind us." I turned to look into the darkness. My grandmother said, "We'll be finding you a new school up ahead."

"Up ahead?" There was darkness up there too, wide and open. "What about everyone else? Are they coming this way too? To the new school?"

"Everyone who can is coming this way. Maybe you'll see them again."

"What if I don't?"

She paused, put down her things, and reached through the dark to get hold of me. I tried to catch a deeper breath, just to calm my dizzy heart. "You will make new friends," my grandmother told me. "They'll be lucky to be your friends. I have left behind a lifetime of friends, sad to say. There'll be as many up ahead as there are behind us."

I took a last look into the darkness at Hungary. I couldn't keep myself from hoping that Zoli and Mary were coming too. My grandmother took my hand again, lifted her bag, and led on.

It was just a few minutes, no more than ten, until we saw a light up ahead, a single bulb, a solitary lamppost. We heard someone say it. My father. "Austria."

As we drew closer to the apron of light—there were only dozens of us now; we seemed to have scattered on our march—I saw Judit lying down on their Persian rug, her knees up, her head cradled by my mother, with Andras between her legs. She was lying right on top of the bird of paradise. The rug was darkening under her.

I was relieved to see my brother there too. His back was to us, and he was peeing.

My father offered to take my grandmother's bag. "What's in this?" he asked. He opened the bag. "What are these?"

"Phonograph records," she said.

"You brought records with you?" he said in disbelief, and rifled through them. They were 78s. He held one up to the light. "*The Barber of Seville*?" He was yelling now.

Judit howled. "This is what you brought?" he said. "*The Merry Widow*?" Then he hurled them, smashing one after another against the lamppost and against the concrete at its base.

"Hey, lunatic man," Andras said. "Get away from here."

"She was taking records to Canada. She wanted *music* there."

"And now she's not," Andras said.

My father stopped. I looked at the scattered bits of record, shiny black shards of sound glinting in the Austrian lamplight. For the first time, I wanted to scream at my father, wanted to hit back.

But then a baby cried. Judit was crying, and my grandmother was crying too on account of the baby.

"Gisela," Andras said as he lifted the little thing waist high. She was still tethered to her mother. "She's a girl. Austrian. *Gisela*."

Judit continued her crying. She was sweating too. And her fiery red hair fanned out from her head, drawing the rest of the light to itself.

"Why Gisela?" my father asked.

But Gisela overwhelmed him with her crying. Her cry was the shrillest. A small crowd had gathered in the light, mostly Hungarians, but also a single Austrian border guard. The little soprano called out to everyone. She was so new and loud, it felt to me that she would lead us now, wherever she needed to go.

THREE

MY GRANDMOTHER AND MOTHER cleaned up the baby with cloths and a little warm water some nuns had brought in a hurry from a nearby convent, and they swaddled Gisela in a soft blanket while Andras cleaned up Judit below. My brother and I watched in horror. I thought Attila would throw up, but then we were treated to a view of Judit's plump breast as she tried to get her little girl to suckle on it, and we marveled at the size of the nipple, round as a sunflower and alive.

Judit needed a rest. She closed her eyes, seemed even to close her ears to the commotion around her. Her heaving chest sagged, emptying itself of living air.

Judit never got up from the foot of that lamppost in Austria. Gisela suckled now with relish from her dying mother's breast, the rug beneath them awash with their broth. The whole world frenzied around the mother and

45

child, who were dazzling in their stillness. Just for a moment, the pair of them made more sense than the rest of us: one of them arriving and the other leaving.

Andras let out a wail. At first I thought the sound had come from somewhere else, somewhere deep in the earth, like something molten.

A flock of nuns swooped down on us. Several of them went straight to Andras. A couple of the others, along with my mother and grandmother, attended to Gisela. And two more of the nuns, big ones, stood between Attila and me and the scene we were watching. They took us each by the upper arm and steered us toward a building around the corner. My nun had a good strong hold on me.

Attila and I turned to take a last look at the foot of the lamppost, and now a second sound rose up, this time out of Gisela, a little trumpet, but with quite a blast, like someone breaking in her instrument. Gisela's face in the lamplight was as red as Mars.

My brother and I were led to an old gray building made of stone, flat-roofed and rectangular. It was ample, but heaving up behind it stood the tower of an even older stone church. A brass sign that said CONVENT OF SAINT ELIZABETH OF HUNGARY arced over the entrance.

"I thought this was Austria," I said to my brother.

"It is, but it used to be Hungary. Not long ago. They speak German and Hungarian here."

The nuns showed us to a large open room called a *lager*, a dormitory with hundreds of cots covered in clean white sheets and nicely pressed wool blankets. There were some people there already and more arriving. Attila grabbed two cots not far from a window and urged me over. Soon, our grandmother joined us, but I couldn't spot our parents, or Andras or Gisela. I was especially wondering about Gisela. I scanned the room, searching for familiar faces, but saw none I knew. I took a second, extra-long look for Zoli and Mary and for my teacher, Mrs. Molnar.

There were no tables set out, but we were handed linen napkins, packets of biscuits and cheese, and milk and wine poured into pewter goblets.

We were surrounded by Hungarians, so it felt like home, though it didn't look like it. Some more nuns stopped by to clear away the remains of our packets and to give us each a small pouch containing chocolates, a toothbrush, a toy-size tube of toothpaste (which I wanted to keep and not open), and a bar of soap.

The chocolates were the best I'd ever eaten, sweet and dense. The wrappers had a picture of Mozart on them.

A voice rang out through the hall, deep and clangy, like a bell. It startled me. We all turned toward a lectern with a microphone that had been set up at one end of the room, and standing at the microphone was a priest wearing a black robe and a great sail of a cap pinched together at the top.

"Today, I am a man without a homeland," he boomed in Hungarian as he raised his arms. "Yesterday, I was Father Tamas, the bishop of Szeged. Today, we Hungarians move as a herd, and our herd has succeeded in eluding the lions to settle peacefully among the lambs. Do not grieve today, my friends, my people. Whatever you have left behind, the Lord will restore to you. Whomever you have left behind, he will protect from harm—if not from earthly harm, then from everlasting harm."

A girl my age a few beds away was staring straight at me. Her mother, beside her, looked stooped and sad and gazed out from under heavy lids pasted with dark blue makeup. Another woman, a brunette of impressive size, tall and strong, sat facing my brother and me, her nightgown hiked up and her grasshopper legs spread wide.

"Look," Attila said to me. "That one is open for business."

The gangling woman had small green eyes like capers. She seemed to know we were talking about her and pulled her ganglies in so she could cover them with her blanket.

The bishop of Szeged clasped his hands in front of him and gazed up to the light, searching for the rest of his speech, it looked like. "The time has come to put sin behind us," he said. "We enter a time of consolation, not vengeance. The Lord of the prophets once said, 'The land is mine.' No one can take away from us that which was not ours to begin with and will one day no longer be theirs. It is our defect, not the Lord's, that we draw lines around things. If the air stood still, we would draw lines around it too. Our lands are those we carry here." The bishop placed a hand flat on his heart. "Those among us here tonight more experienced in the ways of wandering must teach us to carry Mother Hungary in our hearts the way you have carried the Promised Land in yours." Father Tamas crossed his hands over his chest and curled them into fists. He had a way of speaking that made it seem as if the words were written on the sky and he was just reading them, reciting them. "I have left behind me a great church built on a rock in the once picturesque city of Szeged on the shores of the river Tisza, bluer than the Danube. I have left behind me a loyal and true flock, some of whom have scattered today and will not return to the shores of the Tisza. But they walk with us today, those departed, every bit as alive as we are, *more* alive on account of their fate.

"I call upon you of the diaspora to teach us that the land of our fathers and the land of our mothers is here with us today where we sit. Show us how its fragrant green mass is without weight as we set out over the four corners of this earth perchance never again to return, never again to smell the apricot blossoms and blue waters of our Danube and our Tisza.

"And here is what I would say to you today. *End your crusade*. Moderate yourselves. *Moderate yourselves,* I urge you." The bishop raised his fighting fists into the air and then just as abruptly dropped his open hands to his sides, slapping his robe, causing it to ripple like water. "Find peace," he said, "and spread its word and design out from where you have found it. Teach us to find peace. Travel in safety, all of you, and may these be the last of your wanderings. May God bless each and every one of you. Remember always, I implore you, as the prophet Isaiah urged all of us, 'Seek ye the Lord while he may be found.'"

The bishop once again raised his fists, this time to

cover his eyes. Not a person spoke in the room or even whispered. The woman holding her daughter, the one who had been staring at me, had let her go and was weeping black-and-blue tears. Midnight-blue spots stained her white blouse. Her daughter sat with her legs crossed, her bare feet inverted, the soles turned upward as if to catch rain.

The brunette who'd been open for business still had her ganglies folded up as she faced the bishop. I guessed there were no clients for her here, except maybe Attila, who was game for most things.

But my brother was fast asleep, sitting up. I spotted my father and mother in the room now, a dozen cots away from us. There was no sign of Andras or Gisela. I felt terrible dread, felt for the first time how big this night was. I shuddered. My father was devouring several packets of the biscuits and cheese. My mother watched him, then glanced back at the lectern, waiting, it seemed, for the great voice to boom forth again. She looked sad, probably remembering Judit and thinking about Andras and his baby. We were all facing forward, waiting for more, possibly even hoping for it. Attila woke with a jerk amid the murmuring of the place.

The nuns came around with steaming bowls of chicken soup to calm us for the night and with extra napkins to shield our laps from the bowls. They also handed each of us a silver spoon big enough to fit an impressive mouth.

Attila was at his soup immediately, slurping with an ecstasy in his eyes, like someone in love. "Ah," he said.

Then he slurped some more, his eyes closed. "Lique-fied bird," he said. He lifted his bowl and drank the soup down, the first to finish, possibly, in the entire room. Then he set the bowl down on the floor and shifted on his haunches, still smacking his lips, waiting to see what was next. He slapped at something on his collarbone, his eyes casting around the room, searching among the girls. It was as if the bird had remade itself inside him.

Then my brother jumped to his feet. "Look," he said. He was pointing to the front. I stood up to see.

Nuns with musical instruments were arranging them-selves at the microphone where the bishop had stood. One had a cello, one a violin, and one a recorder. A fourth nun clapped her hands sharply until the room went quiet. The cello and violin players tuned their in-struments for just a moment and waited for the leader to nod at them. Then the trio began playing a sad old song. The primary nun closed her eyes, approached the microphone, and sang. I was stunned. It was a haunting, mournful song, sung in Italian. It reminded me of some of my grandmother's records.

"What is it?" I whispered to my grandmother. She was sitting on my cot with me now.

"Goodness," she said. "Just a minute." She stood up too. All over the room, others were standing. The crying woman and her young daughter were standing, and the woman's eyes were welling up.

A flock of sounds swarmed over us in the big room. "Is it a hymn?" I asked. "What is it?"

"It's not a hymn," my grandmother said. "It's an aria, from an opera, by Vivaldi, I think."

The singer's voice was deep as a well, as if a young man lived inside her.

"It's a lament," my grandmother said. "Listen to it." She had her hand on her heart.

The nuns sang several more songs, the cello crooning, the violin soaring, the recorder fluttering like a bird.

"Judit's soul is still here," Attila whispered too loudly. "It's sniffing around."

I got to my feet and gazed all around me. I don't know what I was expecting to find.

As the song wound down, Attila said, "Why does God need to inspire humans to create music just so they can play it back to him? It's all mysterious to me. Are we his concert hall or his radio?"

Our grandmother held up her finger again, warning us to pipe down.

"The music's for us too. Maybe he wants us to enjoy it," I said, but Attila didn't hear me.

"My grandsons, the theologians," said our grand-mother.

The concert finished too soon, and people clapped. Attila and I competed against each other with our clapping. His was sharp and punishing by the end.

People were still arriving and crowding the door, people who hadn't had the benefit of the bishop's speech or the nuns' concert. It made me think that maybe we'd missed some things too. More bombs went off, but their sound was faint, like distant thunder. The field with the mines.

Our grandmother took us to a big open bathroom with more sinks and shower stalls and toilets than I'd ever seen assembled in one place. Attila and I did our business and then washed our hands and faces.

He thought we should use up my toothpaste before we started on his. "There'll be less to carry, my ever-precious love," he said.

I gave it some thought before answering. "But we'd have the same result if we used up your toothpaste first."

He snatched away my bag, but our grandmother said, "Use mine first," and we did. Attila brushed more furiously than usual, spat, and stormed back to the dormitory ahead of our grandmother and me. She ushered me back before returning to clean herself up too.

Before that day, I did not know what a convent was. Attila told me it was a place to get people cleaned up for heaven, if you believed in that sort of thing. I felt very good there, and I told my brother so.

He patted my head and said, "Well, then, if you are an excellent lad, you could grow up to become a nun yourself."

A few minutes later our mother came over to kiss us, but Attila was already out. He had that magic switch that turned off the day and opened up the night with a flick. He was already swinging on vines through the jungle and bellowing, pausing only to pound his chest.

My mother was staring at me and smiling. "How are you doing, my darling love?" she asked. She had such boiling gold hair—it made no sense that she was my mother. Except for her dazzling smile. I had inherited a slightly smaller, darker version of it. She'd passed all the rest of her looks on to Attila—the golden hair, the blue eyes—but she'd omitted her smile. It was the one trait she'd reserved for me. The one outward trait, that is. Attila had very few of her innards.

I asked my mother about the phonograph records, why our father had broken some of them. On came the smile again, with enough amps to light a room.

"You know he gets worked up over the smallest things," she said, "not to mention matters of life and death."

"But we were alive. We'd made it already."

She hugged me hard. "It will be all right, I promise," she said. The hug felt strange, possibly because of where we were and what had happened, all the excitement. It felt new, as if we were inventing the gesture. We floated up, both of us, on the suds of her hair. And then she kissed me and left, pulling the warm air with her.

When the lights went out, I could still feel the coolness of my mother's kiss on my cheek. It was very dark in the room in an absolute way, like space without stars. People sighed, snuffled, grunted, and snored, some nearby, some far across the room, comforting sounds.

But then came a cry from a distant room, followed by a muffled wail, a surrender to full crying. It was a baby. Gisela. Maybe not knowing exactly what she was missing but knowing that it was something. And calling out for it. Andras *oh-oh-oh*-ed her, and I imagined him jiggling her, as he jiggled his own voice to soothe her.

When a nun rolled up a couple of window blinds, the

moon entered, lighting up the carnival of sound and sil-
vering over the sleeping figures like old film. And it hit
me finally. The green eyes of Judit, green as the hanging
soldier's eyes. They would never again take in that light.
All the switches were off now. I began sobbing again like
a baby. I had to pull the covers up over my head before
the X-ray moon exposed my unmanly state.

FOUR

THE NEXT MORNING, we were given fresh napkins, and the nuns spread out across the big room to serve us warm rolls and tea with lemon. I could not see the girl and her mother with the midnight eye shadow. Their cots were empty, the blankets neatly folded. Nor could I see Andras and Gisela. Or the gangly brunette with the caper eyes. Where had they all gone?

My mother and grandmother had left us a little while earlier, and now they came back dressed as nuns, but without the white collars or head coverings. They hadn't brought black clothing to wear for a funeral, so the nuns had helped them out. They were even allowed to tear the garments at the neck to show their grief, as long as the tears weren't too big and my mother and grandmother promised to sew them back up afterward.

57

I thought of where Judit would end up—all those lively colors browned over and dampened down. I thought of how still she would be, the stillness of her in her grave.

Our father came in with bleary-eyed Andras, who was holding Gisela and feeding her a bottle while rocking her gently. He told us the mother superior had asked the groundskeepers to make a little fenced-off area in the graveyard especially for Judit.

"Fenced off?" my mother said, looking a little fearful.

"It's a Catholic cemetery," Andras said, his voice uneven. "This little section will be her own. A little Jewish section, I guess."

Our grandmother took the baby from Andras and continued to feed her the milk. Unlike the night before, Gisela seemed as content as could be.

"I suppose that's what the bishop was saying yesterday," said our father as he raised his hands in the air. "The land is mine, saith the Lord."

"Please, Simon," our mother said.

"It's in the book of Leviticus," he said. "I'm sure it's all right to be quoting the Bible here."

"Can we go see?" Attila asked.

"Yes, but don't wander away this time," our mother said.

Outside and just down the path from the convent walls, a couple of men were driving wooden fence posts deep into the soil, capturing a corner of the graveyard, while two others were digging a hole for Judit to lie in. The black earth gave off a dark fragrance.

"I guess they couldn't take her back home," I said to Attila.

"Of course not," my brother said. "There are Russians there. What I don't know is why we can't go up ahead somewhere to bury Judit. Take her with us—to Vienna, maybe, where there already is a Jewish section."

"Because she died here," I said. "How could we carry her?"

"We won't be walking from here," my brother said. "I'm sure we won't." He closed one blue eye to the sun. He was always doing that: closing one eye at a time in the bright light.

The men working were strong, like soldiers. One was as big as an army truck. He was already down in the hole he'd made, tunneling away, flinging dirt up to the surface. He looked powerful enough to dig a hole for a dozen people to lie in. The man felt our eyes on him and poked his head up. He was coated with an old grime—natural grime that seemed to come from inside him, like a spewing black heart and lungs rather than the dirt of the world.

I soon found myself watching alone. When I turned all the way around, my brother was already halfway across a field beyond the graveyard. He stopped to call to me. "I want to show you something."

"*Again?* I'm not sure about this. What can you show me?"

"*Something,*" he said. "I know this place."

I trotted through the grass toward him. "How can you?" I asked when I got close. "We just got here."

"I know this place," Attila said again. "Trust me."

I couldn't tell where we were heading—back to Hungary, it seemed like. I wouldn't have put it past my brother. The October sky was summer blue, and the sun was extra yellow and hot. I wondered what it would look like in reverse: a blue sun and yellow sky. I preferred the original choice. And the shape of the sun too. Better a sphere than a triangle, say, pointing its light this way and that, searing into things.

As if it had heard me, the sun reared up in the cool sky now and roared. It was too hot.

I remember that moment, that exact moment. Just two days earlier I had been getting over that Septembrous feeling—the end of summer, the beginning of school, the new girl in class, the two new boys, one named Karl, the decimal points, the adjectives: blue, nice, sudden, gradual. Now the sun was spread-eagled across the sky, roaring away, and we had left our home and were running toward something, and I didn't know what.

The field was overgrown but turning to straw and raspy. It felt as if no one had ever walked this way before, no Hungarians, no Russians, no Austrians. But when I caught up with Attila, he said, "There must be as many skulls underneath this land as in the graveyard, if not more. There must be army buttons and spearheads, doubloons and shields, going back to kingdom come."

"Are there girls down there too?" I asked.

"Oh, yes," Attila said. "Think of all that pink love in the ground. Think of it, gone to waste."

There was a little mound up ahead. Attila bent down,

his straight stiff hand shaped like a scythe, and chopped the grass, as if he were scalping it. He studied the clear space to see what might be lying below it.

I stopped and considered letting him continue on his own, but he grabbed my hand. "Don't worry, my ever-present darling," he said. "You're safe with me."

Sheep *baa-ah*-ed in a neighboring field, a shadier, greener one, watching us. They were thick, fluffy creatures, chewing and chewing. Little did they know they were getting themselves primed for sweaters and pots, clumps of them spun into yarn, bits of them lying down with potatoes and carrots.

I wondered what Attila was thinking as he watched the animals with his one eye closed. He held up a hand to block out the light, and the sun stenciled a perfect black hand onto his face.

"Where do you think Judit is?" I asked.

"Dead" was all he said.

"That's it?"

"She'll be going down deep into the ground, all that milk meant for Gisela wasted. She'll be food for worms and little crawly bastards."

"And?"

Attila opened his other icy eye and said to me, "Those sheep over there?" The creatures were still looking at us, even the ones that had turned their bodies away from us. "We are the afterlife of sheep," Attila said, and then he took my hand in his and pulled me forward again.

He led me toward a gate in a stone archway greened over with vines. The letters carved into the arch had worn down with the seasons. There was no one else in sight, no parents, no one. We could still hear the pounding-in of the fence posts in the distance behind us. We stopped before the old gate, but not for long. Attila yanked me along.

"How do you know this place?" I asked.

"I was here with Dad." He was whispering for some reason. "Two years ago. Do you remember the trip he had to take to Vienna to order instruments for his company?"

I recalled that our father had to get special permission to travel and could take only one person with him. I badly wanted to be the one. I remembered the poppy-seed cake I got instead.

Attila was leading me to what looked like heaps and mounds of stones, but with human shapes. The sun was high and the grass even deader here, tall and thorny. We stepped up the pace, almost trotting.

Birds erupted from the grass in front of us and flew off over our heads. I began to feel that it was time to go back, but Attila marched us on. Now I could see better: there were human forms scattered everywhere and piled up in front of us, but stone humans, marble humans, and bronze humans, some outsize, some fierce, some standing and some not, some sweet and loving, with beckoning arms—all of them frozen in whatever big action they were undertaking.

As we approached, the shapes seemed to huddle as if discussing something. Some were toppled, some wore uniforms, their arms thrown over one another's shoulders, looking as if they were leaving a tavern and singing when they had become suddenly encased in metal. One solitary guard lying on his side held up a steely flag ruffled by an old wind, a flag that might have pointed upward to heaven once upon a time but was now pointing instead at a stand of poplars.

"This is the Statue Graveyard," Attila said, as if he were pulling back a curtain. "This was part of Hungary not long ago, this little corner of Austria. Dad showed it to me." He let go of my hand finally.

Over to one side was another heap of bronze figures, and Attila guided me toward it. "I'm not feeling that great," I said.

"It's going to be all right, sweet pumpkin. There's no one alive here." As we drew up to the mound of metal bodies, the head of a woman statue peered out at me from the middle of the pile. Her eyes were blank, the irises hollowed out, her hair in rigid curls, the bangs straight and even.

"Look," I said. "She must have just come from the beauty salon. What are they all doing here?"

Attila put his arm over my shoulder. The ground was damp here, almost swampy. It oozed beneath our feet. He explained that these statues were the writers and leaders and warriors that the Germans hadn't wanted gawking at people in the squares and parks and outside the museums after they invaded Hungary, and now the statues the Russians didn't want had been thrown in with them too. "It goes on like that," Attila said. "It always happens whenever invaders come. They knock down the statues. The

Hungarians grabbed these all up and piled them here before they could be blown up. If the Russians ever leave, then we can knock down *their* statues—Lenin and his band—and put these back up. The powers shift, the borders move, countries rise and fall." Attila tried to sound philosophical and wise as he said all this.

"Is Stalin coming here too, the big Stalin?" I asked.

"He can't come here, because this is Austria now. It was the same during the last century and even before," he said. "Anyway, now there's this place here to save people the trouble of having to cast new hunks of metal every time someone is pushed back out of whatever country."

"Will there be a monument somewhere to the soldiers hanging in the Oktogon?" I asked.

"Not likely. Not while the Russians are in charge."

We paused to study the monuments some more.

"Imagine," Attila said. "Here's where the glories lie. You can have a triumphant battle one day, become hero of the land, get celebrated, have a day named after you, a brilliant funeral arranged for you with the entire nation turning out, have the number one artist carve a fierce and noble likeness of you, and have the square it stands in named after you, for God's sake. Then that same square and the city and the country can be overrun by the Germans or Ottomans or Boogeymen, and suddenly you're dirt. The square is renamed after one of the Boogeys, your chapter is torn out of the history books, the number one sculptor sculpts Lord Boogey, and he gets put up where you once stood. All the heroes who stampeded behind you to victory, who were also encased in bronze and stood in smaller squares and churchyards, get piled in a wagon, you get piled on top, and then you're tossed here."

Attila stepped up to a great sitting figure plonked in the mud, wearing a hood, its arms spread out, a pen of some kind in one hand, a great big bronze book folded under the other, and he said to me, "Do you know who this is?"

He climbed dramatically onto the monument's slippery lap and took the hooded face in his hands, except there was no face in the shadows, or at least I couldn't make it out deep inside the opening of the hood. "It's no one." Attila put his own face into the opening of the hood as if to kiss the figure's lips. His voice echoed inside the small cave. "It's Anonymus," he said, "that's who. It's a sculpture by Miklos Ligeti of no one. Of Anonymus, if you can believe it. Anonymus was the guy who wrote about King Bela III, who lived in the eleven hundreds. But Anonymus was really lots of people who had to hide behind that name to get their work out to the world."

My brother slid off the lap of Anonymus and wiped himself off. He squelched through the mud toward me, then put his wet arm around my shoulders and with the other grandly waved over the looming figures. "Here they are, my beloved boy. Glory be to God and his creatures."

The sight of the noble metal and stone people, all huddled together as they never had before, made me light-headed, as if we had landed on another planet and the air was different, not meant for breathing.

As we turned to leave, I took one last look at the statues all junked together and noticed something I hadn't spotted before. Attila was looking at it too. It was an arm sticking out of the ooze like a sapling, just an arm, and the hand held a bronze book, smaller than Anonymus's book.

"I have to pee," Attila said. "I have to pee violently. Here, come this way."

He escorted me behind the heap of bronzes as if we were sauntering through a salon. When we found just the right spot, Attila went straight to work. I became giddy as I unbuttoned myself and joined him. I started cackling, my pee flying in all directions, but my stream was juvenile compared to my brother's. Attila aimed as high up as he could, on a badly soiled marble shoulder sticking out of the ground, and I joined him.

As we buttoned up, my brother said, "I have one more thing to show you, my turtledove." He led me all the way around to the other side of the hill of bronzes and marbles, then stopped. "Look," he said. He was sober and serious. "Look!" I was already looking. "It's Raoul Wallenberg."

Together we gazed at the man. He was not gesturing, not pointing, not looking at the heavens, merely standing tall, facing us directly. The bronze had blackened. The figure was simple and thin, dressed in a long trench coat.

"Who is Raoul Wallenberg?" I asked.

"He saved everyone. He saved Mom and Dad and me—I was an adorable babe in arms. You weren't even born yet. He was a Swedish diplomat who saved people—

Gypsies, Jews, you name it." My brother explained that Wallenberg had issued fake Swedish passports to people, especially Jews, so the Germans wouldn't take us. He had saved thousands and thousands of people. And then he disappeared.

"What do you mean he disappeared?" I asked. "Do you mean he left?"

"No; he was taken. By the Russians."

I stared again at the statue and wondered whether any Russian statues might end up here beside him. I thought about Papa Stalin without his boots.

"Mr. Wallenberg had helpers, and one of them was Dad's cousin Paul."

"Where is Paul now?"

"No one knows. It's like with Wallenberg. No one knows what became of Paul. He just went away one day and left no forwarding address, but I don't know why, and no one will ever tell me."

I wanted to ask more, but it was too quiet here suddenly. I couldn't even hear birds chirping, and there was something fierce in the bronze eyes of this statue. These things prevented me from going ahead with my questions.

FIVE

WE DIDN'T BURY JUDIT until late in the afternoon. My father said we were waiting for a Rabbi Brandt from Stein, a nearby town, but the man never came. A couple of the nuns weren't sure that the rabbi had survived the war, but a third one said that he had, that he'd returned from a camp, had a small congregation, and was active again.

The former bishop of Szeged, naturally, had heard the news of Andras and Gisela's loss and had offered to conduct the service on behalf of the missing rabbi. He even helped to find six more men to add to Andras, my father, Attila, and me to form a *minyan*. Attila asked whether he and I counted as men. Our father said that we might not, but Andras said it was all right. We counted as men in his book.

Our father looked at his cousin. "They crossed the

border on their own feet," Andras said. Our father put a hand on the back of my neck, then the other on Attila's. He gave us a squeeze before smiling at us.

The girl whose mother had been crying the night before appeared at the graveside. The mother, behind her, looked as if she was waiting for the right moment to spring a leak again.

They were joined by a dozen other people, as well as several nuns, and they all gathered around. My father said it was the smallest Jewish graveyard in the world.

Our grandmother and mother tended to little Gisela, and my father signaled for Andras and me to come and be pallbearers. The four strong men, the fence makers and grave diggers, brought Judit to the door of the convent, and we took over from there. Judit lay on a board and was covered with a blanket. She seemed to shift underneath it.

I was near the front as we marched toward the waiting grave. I struggled like mad to hold up my end, had to reach up high, though I believe I could have let go altogether without much effect. I spotted a lock of our dead cousin's copper hair, which had fallen out of a gap in the shroud. Then a second lock broke free, and the two together flickered like a flame.

My class had taken a field trip not a month before to the Museum of Natural History over on Toth Street. The museum had an exhibit featuring bog people unearthed from the Great Plain, people who'd lain deep in the earth for ten thousand years. A glass case stood at the center of the exhibit. It contained two figures who lay back-to-back in sweet repose. The small man had ancient sprigs of brown hair still clinging to his bony head. But the woman! The woman had flaming hair, lots of it, molten hair, like Judit's, drawing heat from deep down in the earth.

And the flame now passed to Gisela, who wailed with such a redness and fury that, when she got to the bottom end of the wail to take in a breath, the silence burned.

The grimy man leapt into the grave, followed by his partner, and the rest of us were to hand Judit down to them. But Andras wouldn't let go. We all let go, and the board fell into the grave, but Andras clutched his wife like a big rag doll. He seemed to be pleading with her, mouthing words. He turned her upright as if to dance with her, but she was stiffer than I had realized, and he almost lost his footing in the crumbly earth, almost fell into the hole with her. Then the bishop and a nun pulled him back, gently, gently urged him away. Several of the men, including my father and brother, rushed to take over so that Judit could be laid to rest. Andras stared into the earth's black heart as it waited to receive his wife.

What a sound rose out of Gisela as her mother was lowered into the ground! It was a volcano of sound, like the first wail of the world, the wail of the wild, from the land before birth. The sound was so true and pleading that she could have been taken from funeral to funeral to set the tone. A nun, the mournful singer from the night before, tenderly pried the baby girl out of my mother's arms and carried her back into the building, where a warm room and warm milk waited for her.

We were all given hats, and a pretty blond nun named Sister Heidi, who looked like a movie star playing a nun, gave me a Tyrolean hat with a blue feather jutting out of the band. When I didn't take it from her, she placed it on my head herself and tucked my hair under it, as if she were doing a fitting. Her face distracted me from the proceedings.

"Yodel something for us," my brother said. He had on a French beret with one of those little wicks at the top, like a candle.

Even the bishop sported the impressive skypiece he'd worn when he first addressed us, the one that seemed to top off his robe. But he did not have the robe on today, just a long dark coat. My mother and grandmother held on to Andras. We gazed down at Judit, and the water-works began in earnest. How could they not?

The sun, the captain of the skies, blazed away as Father Tamas stepped up. He waded right into the crying sounds. In that voice of his, he said, "You want to ask, 'Haven't I believed in you, Lord? Is the message not getting through, coming from my impure mouth? All this mystery. All this tragedy. What can it all mean?'"

In this place, a priest who had survived and escaped made as much or as little sense as a rabbi who might or might not have survived.

"A true heart," the priest said, "has been laid to rest today even before it was too tired to carry on, long before it was used up. May the Lord bless it, and may he bless ours."

Father Tamas bent his head in silent prayer and stepped

back. Andras broke free from my mother and grand-mother and approached the grave. I thought he might be hiccuping, but even so he whispered the Kaddish: *Yit gaddal, ve yit kaddash, she mei rabba.*

Several people said "Amen," and Andras was the first to shovel dirt into the grave. Others followed suit with shovels, which the grave diggers handed us. Attila hurled down heaping loads and for too long. He had to have the shovel taken away from him and passed to the next person. Sister Heidi dropped in a small bunch of colorful fall flowers. After my shoveling, I stood close to the edge of the grave and didn't want to move. I could make out only the shape of the body by then.

Maybe Judit would be unearthed in a hundred centuries, her hair as red as it was today. Maybe she'd descend with one of the statues—maybe with Raoul Wallenberg, an unlikely couple—searching down in the deep for the earth's pilot light.

SIX

THE NEXT AFTERNOON, the girl whose mother had cried midnight-blue tears told me that Judit was not going to heaven. The girl's soft brown hair was tangly, and she kept sweeping it away from her face on both sides. It was hair wishing it could be something else: drapery, possibly. I was hoping she would smile after what she'd said, which might have meant she'd been joking, but she didn't. She just moved her hair away some more. Her gray eyes flickered through the veil of hair.

"Where's your mother?" I asked.

"Where's yours?" she said.

I told her my parents and grandmother were making arrangements for us to leave.

"Oh," she said, her eyes turned down, as if I'd said she and her mother were being left behind.

"We're all going," I added. "No one's staying here with the nuns. They were just being nice."

The hall was all but abandoned. There was a feeling of movement everywhere else, as if we were at the still center of a carousel.

The girl and I were sitting on our own cots, quite close to each other. She had a powdery scent. Talcum, possibly. But something in addition to the talc that smelled like celery. What the girl had said about Judit still hung between us. She stared with a directness that seemed to give her some kind of authority, as if she was the Commander of Souls.

"Where is Judit, then?" I asked.

The dampest and darkest part of the girl's face was her mouth. She had good fleshy lips, too big for her face but delicious looking. It was the first time I remember wanting to taste someone else's lips. I wanted to take out my marzipan Kaiser Laszlo to show her. I wanted to share my *matryoshka* doll with her. I wanted to put on my Tyrolean hat at a jaunty angle. I wanted to show her Attila's drawing of the fighter plane, possibly pass it off as my own.

"A priest can't send Judit to heaven," she said. "Only a rabbi can. Only a rabbi can send you to heaven. Only a priest can send me."

"But then we'd both end up in heaven," I said, "starting out in the ground."

And now the girl's eyes had turned into luscious mouths too, dark and wet, wanting to say something to me. But they didn't. Instead she huffed herself onto her feet and went off to look for her mother, taking her moist lips with her.

A moment later Attila appeared at the front of the hall and called to me. He was almost hopping, bouncing from foot to foot. It looked urgent. When I joined him, he said, "What? Are you falling for that girl with the banana-string hair?"

"I don't know," I said.

Attila shook his head.

I didn't know what to say. "She has nice lips," I mumbled.

And then the girl reappeared. I was worried she had heard what I'd said or, worse, what my brother had said, but she had a warm look on her face, and I felt relieved.

She sat down on a cot and indicated the one opposite for us to join her. She seemed extra friendly. I saw her smile for the first time, her small, white, even teeth, which seemed to grow out from behind the luscious lips like guards.

"Where's your mother?" my brother asked.

"I'm not sure."

"Has she found some quiet corner to shed a tear in?"

The girl bit her lower lip. She was looking down, but soon she looked up and was smiling again. "You don't look like brothers," she said, but in an approving way. "You look so different." She reached her thin arm forward and touched a small lock of my brother's hair. "It's so pretty," she said. "Handsome, I mean."

Attila pulled back from her admiring fingers and eyes.

"I don't mean..." But her voice trailed off again. She

77

must have been thinking that when the time came my brother would get special permission to share her part of heaven.

Attila saw me staring at the girl still, saw the longing in my foolish eyes. "Give your lips to my brother," he said.

"What?" the girl said, straightening up.

"He's a Beck. He has very distinguished lips. They're better than mine. You'd be lucky to kiss those lips." He was pointing at me, at my mouth.

I wanted to dissolve. I wanted to vanish. Was it possible to die of shame?

The girl saved me the trouble. She stood up and left us in a hurry.

"I'll throw a lock of my beautiful hair into the bargain," my brother said, but the girl was gone. Attila got to his feet. "Now, come with me, my alabaster darling. Come."

"I never want to go anywhere with you again," I said. "If I can help it, I never want to speak to you or see you."

Attila actually looked hurt. He turned to leave the hall the way the girl had.

"Where are you going?" I called after him.

"To the chapel," he said. "The bishop has agreed to chat with us. Stick with me, my one true love. You might learn something." I didn't budge. "I promise never to embarrass you again," he said.

I followed my brother down some dark hallways with many doors, all of them open and the windows in each room open too to let in the fresh autumn air. There was a cot in each room, not much bigger than ours in the big hall, as well as a wardrobe and a small table and chair, as if for a child. There was also a wooden cross on the wall with a bronze Jesus nailed to it. "These are the sisters' rooms," Attila whispered. I knew how hard it was for him to whisper. "This is where they sleep."

We followed a corridor that ended in a great stone chapel. It seemed that all the glorious fervor in this community had been saved up for this building. It was grand, like our temple on Dohany Street in Budapest, but grayer, flutier in shape and tone, flutey like Matthias Church, up in Buda.

The former bishop of Szeged was waiting for us, sitting on what looked like a throne. He looked especially unsuited for the golden seat, as he had on just a charcoal suit and black shirt with a white collar, but no robe, no rings, no skypiece.

He beckoned us with his hands. "Approach, approach." He pointed to a couple of plush footstools, and Attila and I pulled them up and sat before the father.

"Thank you, Your Honor," Attila said, "for the service you gave for our cousin yesterday." He was still almost whispering, but his voice rang out here. "It was special, unforgettable."

I gazed up and all around at the brilliant windows. What a festive place this was. It was raining droplets of light and color—not just over us but over the many paintings featuring glowheads.

Attila said, "My brother and I are here to 'seek the Lord while he may be found.'"

"Your people have been through a terrible time," the

bishop said. "We all have, but your people especially." The father always spoke in an inflated, wondrous way, as if he were trying out new verses for the Bible, as if he knew that God was monitoring everything he said. "We can comfort ourselves with the thought that many who passed nevertheless remain forebears to a new generation. Some, though, I'm sad to say—families whose children perished with them—never got to transect their lines with the other lines of humanity. May the Lord our God look after them especially."

"Judit's line transected," I said, mostly to confirm that I had understood what he was saying. "Isn't that right?"

"It is," Father Tamas said, and he looked up at her in the rafters. I felt reassured. "Still, you've taken a blow," he said and smoothed the hair at the back of my head. His hand was warm and dry. "You've had to leave your home behind."

"I got to say good-bye to Kaiser Laszlo, the monkey, at Gerbeaud," I said. I didn't want to mention the hanging men or the man in the brown suit who'd stood in front of the Urania. Another chill came over me as I thought of the brown hat exploding, the man with the nicely combed hair and very green eyes, the foot that had struck Attila in the dark.

The priest smiled. "I'm glad you got to see the kaiser."

Attila piped up. "Your Honor, may I ask you some design questions?"

"*Design?*" the priest said. He looked ready to smile. "I don't know if I can answer them, but I'll try."

"When the Creator was designing us, at what point

did he decide that the various parts would have more than one function, that he would group functions to-gether in one part?" Attila raised a hand to the side of his mouth, as if he were confiding in the father. "If you think of the parts down below, for instance, they have multiple functions—transecting, as you were just saying, being one of them."

"Yes?"

"And then they are also used for peeing. And they are our alarm clocks. If you didn't have to pee, you could sleep for a week. And it's the other kind of alarm too." He raised his conspiratorial hand to his mouth again. "If you didn't get aroused now and again, there would be very little transecting. If you're a girl, a whole baby has to live and grow in those parts. It's really quite ingenious."

The priest gazed upward toward Judit and the Lord, up into the sprinkling light and color, then down again at Attila, glaring at him now, but with a holy look still.

"Take the mouth," Attila went on. He was pacing back and forth in front of us. "You use it to eat. You use it to breathe. You use it to speak. You use it to smile. You use it to kiss on the cheek, and kiss on the lips and kiss wher-ever..." He paused.

"And?" the priest said.

"And all I mean is that when God was cataloging the various functions of things, I wonder how he came up with these groupings, that's all. The nose smells and snif-fles and holds up glasses. I mean, the mouth could just as easily have been used to smell and the feet to reproduce. The brain could have been placed inside the throat, so that each time you swallowed you'd have a thought. How did these functions get grouped in the ways that they did? Then there are the ingenious groupings having to do with color. Take brown, for instance. You get brown hair, the brown ground, the brown trunks of trees, yellow bananas browning, brown—you know—brown excrement. How did the color get chosen for it? Except that I guess it had to have *a* color—why not brown? But was it a random choice? Conversely, what an ingenious idea to have the *same* thing come in different colors: brown eyes, green eyes, blue eyes, white carnations, red carnations, and such." Attila shrugged his shoulders. "I even wonder if the Lord broke things up into color groups, and if so, how did he do it? Did he start out by breaking them up in other ways? What I mean is, at what point did the Lord decide that grass would be green rather than Mondays being green?"

"Did you say Mondays?"

"I mean, having come upon the concept of colors, did he start out making everything green on Monday, say, then everything red on Tuesday, everything yellow on Wednesday, but I mean *everything,* like a baby God coloring over the lines?"

"A baby God?" the priest said.

"Or maybe it was God's brother." This time the priest did not repeat Attila's speculation. "What about that?" he said. "A brother, maybe. Maybe the less creative one in the family."

The bishop's face was flushed. I thought, possibly, that he was going to leave us. He huffed and was about to say something, but Attila wasn't finished. My brother was like that. His many thoughts lined up at the gate, jostling to get out. He said, "I love the common design of things, like wings, arms, and fins. They all propel creatures, but they also flutter—they enable things to flutter—do you know what I mean? Hummingbirds, black mollies, ballerinas.

"Also," my brother said, rubbing his chin, "did the Lord think up everything at once because he is omniscient? I guess I'm saying, how does that work—being omniscient, I mean? Did he start out, as a baby God, being *somewhat* omniscient? Did he start out as God of the Milky Way, only later to become God of the whole universe?" The priest looked at me. "I guess," Attila went on, "what I'm struggling with is this concept of *always* as opposed to *gradual*. Was it *always* thus and so?" Attila had a fierce, determined look on his face, a look that said, *Help me with these riddles or I shall surely die.* "I commend the Lord," he went on, "for his choice of color for blood, an impressive crimson. It says, 'Alarm!' It says, 'Stanch my flow. I cannot be a river flowing out into the round red sea.'

"And then there's the centipede—the millipede! Surely this is someone's idea of a joke. All right, eight legs, like a spider, or eight tentacles, like an octopus, or none, like a snake, but a hundred, a *thousand?* They were created with holy tongue in cheek, were they not? As was the giraffe. Hmm . . . let's give an animal a three-story neck and decorative little body. And the ostrich and the warthog—they're more in the humor column. And what about the snake? Is that really a finished animal? It's just a tail attached to a head."

My brother raised his inquiring arms to Judit and the Lord. "If heaven is so fascinating, why do God and his angels spend all their time staring down at us? What would they do without us? What did they do *before* us? Is there such a thing as *before?*" He dropped his hands to his sides the way the priest had done during his sermon. And then Attila raised a "eureka" finger in the air. It was his finest performance. "Before all *this* got under way," he said, "if there is a before, whatever *this* is, God must have been looking out at nothing, and he must have thought, 'Why not have *something?*' And what a thing to dream up, too. Life! Life's the most clever currency of all, isn't it?" Attila closed his eyes, but then he opened them again. He looked first at me and then at the priest. "Oh, yes. It's because everyone who has it—*every thing*—wants to keep it, if they have any sense left. So it's powerful to make life, powerful to risk it, and powerful to destroy it. Yes, it is," Attila said, "as you yourself were saying, sir." He paced back and forth in front of us again. "Very powerful, very tempting, very delicious in a way. If you can't put things right—if you can't make your own life work—then taking someone else's life makes a lot of sense. And it gives you the same kind of thrill, the same kind of power—*almost*—as someone who can make life, make babies, make countries. How great it is to knock them down." His voice quieted down. "Gellert," he said. "The hill in Buda is named after him. Gellert Hill. The bishop in Budapest. He was like you, sir, a bishop. He brought Christianity to Hungary, but they put him in a spiked barrel and rolled him down his hill, filling him full of holes. Think of how clever it was even to invent the spiked barrel. Think of how pleased his tormentors were to have come up with the idea. You have to be smart and inventive to devise evil deeds, just about as inventive as when you devise good ones. That's all I can say."

The priest said, "All *I* can say is that it's a good thing we're the only planet in the galaxy with life on it. There'd be plenty of trouble if we weren't. There's plenty of trouble as it is."

I looked up and all around me again, as the good father had done earlier when he was searching for inspiration. I was admiring the celestial community of seraphim, cherubim, and glowheads. I had a question too, which I'd been holding, and since there was a lull in the proceedings, I thought I might go ahead with it. I said, "I'm wondering what seraphim and cherubim do."

Father Tamas looked relieved. "The seraphim and cherubim," he began, "are agents of the Lord. Messengers, really." He looked up into the rafters with me but didn't finish. Attila looked up as well.

Shuttling up to heaven and back was surely what made you a glowhead. The seraphim, cherubim, and glowheads floating up into the air—these must be added to the things that fluttered.

Father Tamas rubbed his eyes and head in the headachy fashion of adults. "Excuse me," he said as he rose from the golden chair. I rose too. Attila was already standing. "I know you boys have been traumatized. You've lost your homeland and friends; you've left behind so much that you love."

"Oh," Attila said.

What the father didn't understand was that, for my brother, everything was a game, one in which the players always hoped they were running loveward but couldn't be sure. The best thing was that all the players got to ask as many questions as they wanted.

On the way back, my brother stopped to tell me, "It's a good thing God was a realist. You could have been designed by Picasso and had your ear nailed to a wall and your dick hung up on a fluffy cloud."

The lack of answers from the priest had upset my brother. "Let's face it," he said. "God was the Creator, and he created *something,* but the rest was a mess." He was whispering too loudly. We were passing the nuns' rooms, glancing into each one. "He was the Creator. He was not the Maintainer. You have to wonder sometimes why the Lord got started in the first place," he said. "Why bother? Especially since he could *foresee* everything. I guess he had to. It would be sad if you were Creator of the Universe but decided not to go ahead with any creations."

"Try to be quiet," I said as we stepped up our pace. I was peeking into each room to look for a slightly more glamorous one, maybe one with gold curtains or festive lighting or even just a pair of red gloves left on the little table.

And then Attila stopped in the corridor. "Do you know what?" he said. "The Lord must have foreseen the Boogeymen, as I said. He must have foreseen the Statue

Graveyard. He must have foreseen Hitler and Stalin. He could have hurried along the process before the lion and the lamb got to lie down with each other and saved people so much unnecessary suffering. He could have made some white mothers give birth to black babies, but not *always*. It would be random. Maybe she gives birth to a giraffe. Do you see what I mean?" I shook my head no. "Why don't dogs give birth to cats?" he said, and he slapped me on the chest with the back of his hand— quite hard, actually. "Do you see what I'm saying? Help us out a little, O Lord. You already had a good idea by making people have to mate to have a child. A very good idea, actually, possibly your finest one. But why not go one step further?"

I tried to continue walking, but my brother wasn't having any of it. I said, "And what happens once the lion and the lamb lie down together?"

"You wouldn't need to mate with anyone anymore, that's what. It would all be quiet and serene."

"And would that be the end of all species?" I asked. "Would that be paradise or death or whatever—the *end?*"

My brother considered my proposition. We walked five more steps, but he stopped us again. "Good one, my tiny brother. No, we wouldn't need to mate. We'd be perfect by then. We could be self-pollinators, like some plants, I believe. You could just make yourself pregnant, lie around all day, and feel up your own special places."

"That would be paradise for you. But then there would be no one to impress."

"Don't be rude, my tender and small brother. It's just another plan, a suggestion, that's all. We'd be in a place that would not require a redeemer. We would never need another flood to wash away the filth and degradation." Attila was still thinking very hard.

"Then why would we need more babies?"

"Oh, dear Lord, we *wouldn't,*" he said. "We have babies to steer us toward perfection. We wouldn't. No cross-pollination, no self-pollination. I have taught you well, my ever-present darling." He gripped my face like a vise and kissed the top of my head.

Then it came to me. "Maybe God is *still* a baby," I said.

My brother froze. He gripped me even tighter. "What did you say?"

"I said"—my voice was distorted as I squeezed another thought out of the vise—"maybe there's a ratio of years between Creator and human, a million to one, say." We had just completed ratios in school. "Possibly the Lord is a little older. Kindergarten Lord. It would explain some things."

My brother further tightened his lock on my face, if that was possible. I couldn't say another word. He kissed me on the forehead this time. "What thoughts you have, my raven-haired beauty." And he kissed me again on each cheek.

As the blood returned to my face, all this talk about life and death made me think that I would never see Judit again or the grim ladies with their bright tree in the painting called *Christmas 1903*. I might not even see the girl with the delicious mouth or the tall woman with the caper eyes, and a man with combed hair might swing through my dreams for quite some time to come.

When we got back to the big hall, many people, including our family, had returned and seemed to be packing their few belongings. I noticed that the cot next to mine, where the girl had sat that morning, was stripped of its linens and that the girl's little sack of belongings was gone. Her mother's cot was also bare. I was quite sad about it. I wished my brother hadn't said anything to her. I never did see the gangling woman again.

Our parents told us that we were making an early start tomorrow and that we should eat our entire dinner before getting ready for bed. Andras wouldn't be traveling with us, our mother told us. He would be going somewhere else. We saw them, Andras and his daughter, with our grandmother at the far end of the hall. He was bouncing the little redhead too hard, I thought. Our grandmother took over the baby.

"Where are they going?" Attila asked.

"Somewhere else," our mother said again. "We won't be traveling together."

"Where are we going, and where are they going?" he said again, huffing. The question was powered by his annoyance with Jesus and Father Tamas.

"We're going to Paris first," she said. Our father glared at her. "But just for a visit," she quickly added. She was fixing Attila's collar.

"What about them?" I asked this time.

"They are going to Israel, my love." She turned to fix my collar too, though it was already fine.

89

Attila and I went over to our cousins to say good-bye, and for the first time I was stabbed by the blade of this departure, wounded more deeply than by our escape from home. Maybe at first all the excitement of it—the minefield, the hot darkness—had distracted me.

I couldn't even look at Gisela. Andras gave me a snap-shot of Judit, who appeared rosy, even in black and white. I hugged him around the waist, and he clasped the back of my neck with both of his hands. I made my way to the bathroom, where I stayed, staring at the photo of Judit until I could be sure that Gisela and Andras had left.

Later, in the big room, I waited stupidly for the girl with the delicious-looking mouth and her tearful mother to return, but of course they didn't. They'd fled, after tak-ing the trouble to banish Judit from heaven.

Attila asked our grandmother why anyone would go to Israel, but when his head met the pillow, the question got switched off. What a freak of nature my brother was. He was awake or he was asleep, a Hungarian one second and Tarzan the next, winter one day, summer the next. Spring and fall were not his seasons. There was nothing gradual about him. No dawn, no sunset. But to me big things seemed gradual. Winter didn't just switch off. Neither did the sun. It took the sun a whole evening to hand over the light to the moon. Sometimes I don't know how the two of us could have been brothers, Attila and I. We were the Adjective Brothers: Sudden and Gradual.

When the lights went out, I waited, as awake as I could be, among the breathers and snorers. I got up and snuck over to the window. I looked up at the clear, star-flecked sky, following its dots and joining them into the dippers and the butterfly of Hercules and the braid of Ally. Just then my grandmother put her hand on my shoulder, and I jumped. She was like a stealthy assassin. She whispered for me to be quiet, crossed out her mouth with her finger. She gazed out the window with me, seemed to be studying the stars, as I'd been doing.

She said, "Some of those stars out there are gone now."

I turned toward her to see if she was mocking me, possibly, but she had a tender look in her eyes. "Just how do you mean?" I asked.

"I mean they're so far away that they sent out their light many, many years ago, and the light is only just arriving, even though the star has extinguished itself since. All the light you see is old at the very least, but more likely ancient."

"Ancient light," I said.

"And other light, new starlight, is being sent out right now, which we *can't* see—which, by the time it gets here, we won't be around to see, not even you."

I asked what that meant. Did it mean that Ursa Major's leg was older than its other parts, that some of it formed earlier, *before* it was a bear? Was there another bear or a fish up there still waiting to be born?

"Yes, possibly," my grandmother whispered into the crown of my head. "Now, why don't we go to sleep? Why don't you go to bed?"

"I will," I said, gazing up at the prickling darkness. "But what about the North Star? What if it goes? How will sailors find their way across the sea?"

"I don't know," my grandmother said.

"What about people in love—*lovers*—walking along as they do, holding hands as they look up at the stars? Do they know it's old light they're seeing, that the source of the light is gone?"

"I don't think they worry about it," she said.

"What about the sun? What about *our* star?" I said. "Will people in some distant place be seeing its light long after we can't see it anymore?"

"Maybe, yes, maybe."

I wanted in the worst way to wake Attila to tell him what I had just learned from our grandmother. But I didn't want to stir him up, so I decided not to.

SEVEN

I WOKE UP TO piano music. My grandmother was sitting on my cot, holding my hand, her eyes closed, swaying to the lilting sound. Beautiful Sister Heidi, the one who'd given me the hat, sat with her back to us, playing the upright piano at the front of the hall. Attila was still asleep. My grandmother's pinkie ring was digging into one of my fingers. It was the famous old turquoise ring I had always admired and twirled whenever I could.

"It's Beethoven," my grandmother whispered. "His *Waldstein* sonata."

I sat up, and she squeezed my hand. "Listen to it," she said.

"I'm listening."

"Wait for it."

Sister Heidi's shapely form moved inside the bag of her habit, her body stirring the rough cloth from inside. But the playing was as nice as the player.

My grandmother was still squeezing my hand—too hard, I thought, which is what people seemed to be doing to me lately. "Listen to it," she whispered again. "Beethoven is saying, 'Behold the mountain, delight in the rose, rise out of yourself.'" My grandmother closed her eyes again as the sister turned the keys into thunder makers. "Listen to it," my grandmother said with closed eyes. "Listen to the man."

"The woman."

She opened her eyes. "The man and the woman both. The truth of it. The truth of the composer. 'Crush your enemies,' it is saying to some people. 'Rise up,' it is saying to others. 'Believe in yourself,' it is saying to still others. You can see why the composer sometimes sent these fists of music flying at you. And not just fists—his lips, his eyes, his heart. Great sounds are like that. They have their own language. 'Behold the mountain' sometimes sounds like 'Be the mountain.'"

I kept staring at Sister Heidi, listening and staring. And finally, when she rose from her bench, she looked shy, alone, as if Beethoven had left her. For a moment, she didn't turn to face us, but then she did. She smiled, bowed her head, and left too suddenly. My face felt hot. Attila had slept through it all.

My grandmother went to get me a roll with cheese and jam, together with a cup of warm milk. Then she took her seat beside me again while I spread apricot preserves on my roll.

"Can I help you?" she asked.

I shook my head. It felt very warm in the room. I

could feel myself salting up again and stuffed some of the warm roll into my mouth. Finally, I said, "Mamu, that man we saw hanging at the Oktogon—"

"Please try not to remember him, my darling." My grandmother's eyes were caramel and soft.

"He was the eighth dead person I've ever seen," I said. "The first seven were hanging men too. And then there was the ninth, the smoking man. The tenth was Judit—maybe the eleventh, if you count the foot that hit Attila. The person it would have been attached to." I looked down into my lap, took another bite of my sweet roll.

"That is far too many," my grandmother said. "Even one is too many for such a young man to see."

"How many dead people have you seen?" I said with a full mouth.

"I've seen too many too."

"How many? Who?" I took another bite out of my crusty roll, stuffed my mouth.

"My dear parents," she said. "My dear husband—your grandfather, whose name you have. How he would have loved you, especially. You look just like him. But let's stop. Please, try to forget these dead people, especially that sad last man hanging, and especially Judit. I know it's hard, but try, my darling."

"Did the people who killed the man that was hanging know who he was?"

"Please eat your breakfast."

"Did they?"

"How could they? They killed him because of what he stood for, the colors he was wearing. Those land mines in the field were intended for anyone crossing the field, not because someone was saying, 'I don't like you, Robert Beck,' but because to them you are one of the others. It's just the colors they were hanging at the Oktogon."

I looked outside the window at the bright sky and the clouds. What if clouds reflected things, carried pictures of things, pictures of souls entering into them, one at a time, each adding a drop of color—red Judit, red combed hanging man, brown smoker—until they rained down on other places?

A diesel bus soon pulled up in front of the convent. It was to take the rest of us to Vienna, and from there another bus was to get us to Paris, where my great-aunt Hermina, my grandmother's sister, was waiting.

I was feeling as if I could have stayed a little longer among the nuns. I thought I could have continued with school there, possibly, found the right skypiece, like the one worn by Father Tamas, and learned how to make speeches. Some of my friends might eventually join us to fill out the class.

Sister Heidi appeared again. Her presence cheered me up. Her eyes were cornflower blue in this light. I was glad I had put on my hat. When she saw me staring, she stepped over to hug me, and I took extra long over it. She seemed as soft as I'd imagined under the habit, but smaller, and she had a clean fragrance. I wanted to know about her. I wanted to know if she had red shoes stashed away somewhere, or red gloves. I wanted to ask her if she thought Judit had made it to heaven, at least to her section of it, but I didn't have the nerve and wasn't ready for the answer to be a disturbing one.

Heidi was wearing her coif but not her white neck band, and for the first time I got a good look at her neck. It was the whitest, most supple neck I had ever seen. It was what marble was trying to be when it was trying to be flesh. My eyes traveled up and down the soft white column. What messages could it be carrying from her heart to her head and back to her heart again? What messages flew in through the blue windows of her eyes?

My own heart danced wildly in my chest.

"Where are you going to go?" Heidi asked.

It took me a moment to find my bearings. "I don't know," I said. "Paris first, but then Canada, I think. I wish I could stay here and have my family send for me eventually."

Sister Heidi must have found this to be the funniest remark she'd ever heard, because she laughed up a storm, laughed until she hiccuped. Her magical neck spasmed with it.

Then she straightened herself out and said to me, "The meek shall inherit the earth." She smiled, turned, and strolled away. Is that what she thought I was, then? Meek? My head was hot under the Tyrolean hat. I took it off to smooth back my hair.

Attila came up behind me. "What's that one's name?" he asked.

"Sister Heidi."

"That's the same one from before, right?"

"Yes. Before."

"Wow, she would be the Virgin I'd select for the

Second Coming. And she's a nun! She wouldn't ask questions about the mystery of it all. What did she tell you?"

"She told me the meek shall inherit the earth."

"Great," Attila said. "Very wonderful and very great. Is that what she is? Is she meek? If that's meek, then take me to your leader."

Attila and I got on the bus, and I turned to the window right away to look for Sister Heidi. But I knew now that she was out of reach, just like the girl with the stringy hair and exceptional lips. We were not at a place where we could stay or even visit again. We were at a place we had to leave, and Sister Heidi and the girl belonged only in this place.

Back home, bombs were dropping or rising out of the ground, saying who would sit on the throne, who would lie in the cemetery, who would be moved to the Statue Graveyard, and who the meek would be. But how could we go toward something that was only a word? *Canada*. It was just a sound. It had no shape or weight. You could not take its temperature. It was hard to imagine Canada as a place where people were eating eggs or taking a walk or hugging nuns or playing cards. If God switched off gravity, maybe we wouldn't be bound to Canada or Paris or Utah or here, and we could fly where we wanted or just tread the air, become fluttering things.

I kept straining to see Heidi by the convent door. I couldn't get over the feeling that I was seeing things for the last time. It came over me in waves, like the memory of Judit.

As we settled onto the bus, I carefully placed my satchel in the rack overhead. Attila threw himself down beside me.

A woman was getting on the bus just then, all decked out, her shiny long brown hair hanging and bouncing, her pearl earrings dangling and a pearl necklace curving down from her neck to her black dress.

I stared at my brother, extra hard. I asked him, "What will you do in the Wild West?"

He tapped his chin with his index finger. He was taking my question very seriously. "I'll become a cowboy rabbi," he said. "And a fur trader as well. Beaver and otter and silver fox, I think." He patted me on the head. "And you can pursue your dreams of becoming a singing nun." I shoved his patting hand away.

Our father had been a tool and die maker during the war because he couldn't become a lawyer. By the time he was ready to go to university, Jews could not be admitted. I asked Attila if he thought Dad would be a tool and die maker again.

Attila looked over at our father, then shrugged his shoulders. Sunlight beamed into the bus now. My brother shut his one eye against it.

"Ah, the Brothers Karamazov," our father said. He startled me. He was checking our things above our heads too and was standing over us.

"I don't know what that means," I said, and I looked at my brother.

Our father patted me on the back of the head. I had an excellent head for patting. He then made himself comfortable opposite his mother and ours. They were smiling warmly, our mother especially.

A minute later, my brother was asleep again in the seat beside me, his grasshopper legs like the gangling woman's, up and folded back beneath him. I wondered if the Lord had considered making retractable limbs for when they were not in use. I was surprised Attila hadn't put his feet up on the empty bench in front of us.

"Are you not worried?" my mother said to my father.

"Yes, but I'm happy to be on my way to something new."

My mother stepped across to sit with my father. She took his hand in hers. "You *are* worried. Please don't be so anxious," she said. "When you're anxious, everybody is anxious."

"People are quite adept at being anxious on their own," he said.

"They get *more* anxious," said Mamu, "when you go mad."

"I'll replace your records," he said.

My grandmother smiled warmly, brought her hand up to her mouth. But what she said was, "Records are just records. A child was being born right before our eyes."

"And Judit was dying," my father said and covered his face with his hands.

My mother cradled his head and told him it was all right. It was not his fault. A few minutes later, he was asleep.

I stared again at Attila—he and I, the two musketeers. We'd left plenty behind, but whatever was ahead, we would overcome it. First, though, we needed our rest.

EIGHT

THE BUS STOPPED FOR a short time at a place called Eisenstadt, jolting my brother and me awake. From the window we could see that the town had an impressive church and railway station, but it looked like a country town in every other way. Carts and wagons rolled in with their chickens and milk and cheese. In the center of the main street stood a single fountain, where a bronze chubby naked boy peed out water to anyone who wanted some. Only the pigeons seemed interested.

We'd had our feet up on the empty bench seat opposite us on the bus, but a young gentleman got on and chose to sit across from us. So my brother and I straightened up. A handful of other passengers who looked as if they might have been farmers boarded, carrying bulging sacks. Across the aisle, our father was asleep, but not our mother and grandmother, though they looked hypnotized by the ride.

The gentleman said something to us in German, but when we didn't answer he switched to Hungarian. He said, "Are you going very far?" I told him our destination, and he said cheerfully, "I'm going to Paris too, finally!" He sounded for a second like one of us, a boy himself.

"Have you always wanted to go?" Attila asked.

"I've been there twice, but it has been difficult these past couple of years."

We nodded that we understood, and he looked us over, as we did him. Where had he crossed the border? Had he crossed a minefield too, or had he known a better way? The gentleman had an elegant Old World look about him. He was dressed in a gray three-piece suit with a herringbone pattern, a starched white shirt with French cuffs, and a black Ascot cap, which he'd removed with a flourish when he greeted us. His hair was thick and as black as the cap. He carried only a black leather briefcase, which he tucked under his arm and kept secure on the seat.

He introduced himself as Peter Halasz and offered us his hand.

My brother took it firmly. "We're the Beck brothers," he said, eyeing our companion. "Attila and Robert. Robert was named after our grandfather. I was named after the warrior, the ruler."

"Of course."

"The Hun," Attila added, and the man smiled.

The bus departed Eisenstadt and bounced along the road. The countryside looked like Hungary's. I would not have guessed we were in another country except for the odd sign in German, sometimes with Gothic lettering to give it a higher feel.

The bus slowed slightly for a man riding a white horse on the road. He passed right by our window. "Nice horse," my brother said with authority. "Fine leather saddle."

Was this our future as cowboys? It dawned on me that the saddle separating the man from his horse was made of cowhide. He was sitting on the crumpled-up hide of a cow and wearing a deerskin vest and a lambswool hat. What a piling up of animals was there!

Suddenly I wished I had put on my brown loafers instead of the black lace-ups I was wearing. The loafers weren't as nice, but they were roomier. I wondered if I'd left them by the front door at home, or underneath my bed, and what the Russians would do with them—throw them out or give them to someone who could enjoy their roomy comfort.

For a short time, Peter Halasz looked out the window, as we were doing. Our mother kept an eye on us and flashed her characteristic smile. It was hard not to smile back at her many times a day.

"What do you do?" Attila asked.

"Guess," Peter Halasz said. The man didn't know what he was getting into.

"You're a lawyer," Attila answered.

"No."

"A professor?"

"No."

"A government official." Peter shook his head no. "A doctor." No. "A chemist." No. "A manager of a department store—the manager of Kossuth's." Peter shook his head. "An army officer, a milliner, a sommelier, a volcanologist, a diplomat, a landlord, a crystal physicist, an engineer, a researcher in textiles." No, no, no.

"I'm—" Peter Halasz was about to say, but my brother wouldn't let him.

"A haberdasher," Attila said, "an archaeologist, a philatelist, a conductor, a fabulist, a playwright, an opera singer." Attila was red-faced. I dared not guess in case I got it right, nor did our mother, who was listening. "A botanist, a zookeeper, a Communist spy, a film director, an architect, a tool and die maker, a millwright, a linguist—"

"I'm a master perfumer," Peter cut in.

"What?" Attila said. He seemed ready to jump out of his seat.

"I am an expert in scents." He pointed to his nose.

Attila and I were both impressed and curious. "Of course," Attila said, slapping his own head. He looked at me, then back at our companion. "You're going to Paris!" He slapped himself again. "But a master perfumer," he said. "I've never heard of such a thing."

"You have heard of more professions than I was expecting," the gentleman said, "but, yes, that's who I am."

"I'm glad we got that out of the way." He pointed to his nose.

Our grandmother was staring at Peter Halasz. She was ready to hear more too.

"I smell heather from a field coming up ahead," he said. "I smell paprika. Hay for horses and flax for linen. I smell coffee from a thermos up near the front of the bus. You must smell it too."

We both nodded. We studied the man's cheerful face. Our mother was doing the same now.

"I smell some pickled herring, a single serving, most likely, not much more. I smell its onions and salt. You might smell it as well."

Attila stood up to see if anyone was eating. I did too. There was an old woman hunched over something, an open jar, but it was not easy to tell what was in her jar, which she guarded on her lap.

"But the difference," Peter said, "is that two days from now, I will smell the fish oil flowing under the skin of the person who's eating it, settling there."

Our mother shook her head, but she smiled some more.

"I smell earth on board," Peter went on. "Black earth, not much, earth drying on boots, almost certainly farmer's boots."

"Yes, but you got on the bus with farmers," Attila said.

Peter ignored my brother and closed his eyes. His nose became his eyes. "I can smell the powder of moths' wings."

"What do you mean?" Attila asked. "What does it smell like?" He was sitting right up in his seat, all set to hunt for moths.

Peter explained that it isn't really powder. It only looks like powder, and butterflies have it too. The powder is made of tiny scales, cells like our own skin cells. But in moths the scales protect it from water and abrasion, and they are slippery so that moths can escape a spiderweb. "I can smell male moths and butterflies," he went on, "because they can turn on a scent with their scales, to attract a mate. I can smell the scent of sex in insects. You can imagine it in humans."

Attila looked alarmed. He sat back in his seat.

"I can gauge the humidity in the atmosphere, the ratio of water particles to air, within a single percentage point," the man said. "I smell microbes, spores, pollen, the feces of mites, and scents all the way up the ecosystem, including those of large mammals—whales. I can tell if water particles have passed through the spout of a whale or fallen unimpeded to the earth.

"When I go to the theater, I smell the cedar of fur closets, citrus aftershave, the rose note of Chanel Number Five—the five-petal *Cistus* rose—which conjures up the boyish flappers of the 1920s, clean and simple. I smell the filaments of wool, whether from Highland sheep or the merino lamb of Vermont's rolling hills and the green valleys between."

"What are you?" Attila said. "You're a freak. You're like a fox or a bloodhound."

"Something like that," Peter Halasz said, "except foxes and bloodhounds can't name what they're smelling, even if they have an instinct for what it might be."

"It's a gift," I said, only because I thought my brother might be insulting Mr. Halasz.

"It's a curse and a gift," Peter said.

"You have a sixth sense," our mother said.

"Not a sixth one, just an outsize version of one of them—outrageously outsize. I'm like a blind man, a deaf mute."

We all stared at Peter's nose as if it were an instrument, an artifact—the Magic Nose. He raised his fingers to cover it.

"You're like a superhero," Attila said. "I wish I had that. You're like Superboy. But you're Noseboy. You could be Noseboy."

"That's why I'm a perfumer. You can see why."

I nodded, but Attila said, "You could do so much more—fight crime or save people."

"Yes, possibly."

Our mother and grandmother both beamed. They seemed to want to say something, but they didn't.

The bus rolled toward Vienna. We were on a bigger road now, a highway, not rocking quite as much in our seats.

Attila said, "Can you smell your own heart beating, Mr. Halasz? Can you smell the red flow of it, the iron of it?"

"I don't need to smell it," Peter said. "I still have other senses." He cupped an ear and put a flat hand against his heart.

"You're amazing," Attila said. He was admiring our companion as if we were actually sitting with Superman or Batman or Flash.

"I smell honesty," Peter said. "I smell eagerness, antic- ipation. I smell charisma, the musk of it. I smell fear. I smell fertility." Attila's eyes widened. "You might smell the coming of rain the way I do," Peter said, "but I smell more. I smell the earth opening itself up to receive it."

I wanted to ask whether Peter could smell old light, the ancient light arriving from the stars, but I didn't want it to be a silly question, so I held back.

NINE

IN VIENNA, WE WERE once again led into a great hall, which held hundreds of other Hungarians and hundreds of cots. The immense hall could have been in a school or a hospital—I wasn't sure—but it seemed so suited to the purpose of receiving people that I imagined that was what it was for. Vienna must receive many people all the time was what I imagined. The hall had a vaulted ceiling hulking over it, and its wooden ribs made me think of a fairy tale, though I wasn't sure which one. There were no glowheads of any kind up there.

I was impressed with how many of us had made it out. Right away, after an official looked at some of Peter Halasz's papers, he was allowed to leave. He waved at us from a far door. I thought we'd be traveling to Paris together and was sad when I saw that we wouldn't be. I'm sure Attila was too, but he didn't say.

It was a new trend: people coming into our lives and leaving just as quickly.

I felt a twinge when I thought about Judit. She seemed even farther away, gone for months, even a year.

Attila told our father all about Noseboy, and he asked if we were sure. Of course we were sure, Attila told him, and our mother nodded in agreement.

"What if he was a fake?" our father asked. "A good one, a smart one, but a fake?"

"What do you mean?" I said.

"What if he was an actor?" our father said. "Or insane?"

"Enough, Simon," our mother said, and she glared at him. He glared back. Her glare was always less effective than his because you could tell she had a smile waiting behind hers.

"What if he was a *genius?*" Attila said. "A freak, like Mozart?"

He looked ready to hit our father, who backed down. "Well, it's possible. Not likely, but possible."

"How likely was Mozart?" Attila asked, and he slapped at the air. My brother was a real slapper and puncher.

This new building was not as welcoming and warm as the convent had been. We were given nice food, rounded off by more nice chocolates, in fact the same Mozart chocolates, but the place felt more regimented. These Austrians seemed mostly to have a processing job to do. There was a single standout, a boy no older than Attila who wheeled a cart around the room and stopped at every child, giving each of us a package. When he got to

110

us, he said, "Pez," and then in labored Hungarian told us that Pez candy was invented in Vienna. He handed Attila and me one container each. They were quite wonderful—figures from *The Wizard of Oz*. I got the Tin Man. I held it tightly in case the figure Attila got was not as good, like Glinda or Toto. But he got an excellent one too, luckily: the Scarecrow. Within seconds, we were lifting the heads of the dispensers and pulling the delicious rectangular candies out of their necks. Attila wanted to bang the heads together, but I put mine away before we could get under way.

Then a girl came by our cots. She was as blond as Attila and dressed in a green-and-white gingham dress. The outfit was very tight, to bring out the figure eight of her form, except she was much smaller on top than on the bottom, so the eight came out like two plus six rather than four plus four. She floated by too slowly and wanted to linger near my brother, but he gave off his blue glare. Some girls didn't know when they were flying too close to the sun. Attila half turned away from her, paying more attention to me, actually. I was worried he would offer her to me. He ignored her outright, and she drifted away.

Before we settled in for the evening, each of us, including Attila and me, including our parents and grandmother, was taken into a curtained-off booth and examined by a doctor and nurse—our noses, throats, ears, and armpits, and even our nether parts—the parts made for all those functions, as my brother had pointed out. When the doctor was down there, I told him all about Peter Halasz, what a chance the doctor had missed not giving the man's nose a good going-over, but the doctor didn't even speak Hungarian, and the nurse spoke only a little.

Even worse, these medicals took my blood, had me pee into a bottle, and gave me a shot of vaccine, which, for all they knew (because they didn't ask in any language), I'd already received back in Budapest. I was then taken off for an X-ray of my chest and had to hold my breath for it, something the technician demonstrated rather than told me while they got ready. One of them even turned to take a gulp of coffee to fortify himself.

My brother and I met in the giant bathroom. I saw my brother enter one toilet stall, and I ran to get the one beside him.

"What a strange thing," he said. His voice echoed here.

"What is?"

"This inward and outward movement," he said. "Food in, food out, water in, water out, air in, air out. Turning all this fine food into crap. Turning enticing, fragrant things into stink. You have to wonder why it's necessary. You have to think there must be a lesson in it somehow."

As Attila was talking, I was thinking again of Judit, in the ground, and of the sheep we had seen, how my brother had said we were their afterlife, but possibly just the afterlife of things, not of the light from dead stars. I wasn't sure. "It's a cycle," I said. "Everything's a cycle."

"Yes, and the cycle is always the same," my brother said. "We just don't always see it. Different food, same crap; different lives, same ground. Holy lives, poor lives, long lives, short lives, glorious lives and inglorious."

We sat, then, in silence. The radiator ticked in the bathroom. It was quite warm. There was a sound like a towel being snapped and then some pattery footsteps.

By the time we were finished, washed, fed, and sitting out front on our new cots, dressed in the gowns we'd been given, which were now doubling as nightshirts, my brother and I looked like swashbucklers who'd been stripped of our capes, swords, and three-cornered hats.

Our father was having words with an official as he held out our papers, but a larger, more commanding official stopped by us, and my father shrank into a meek and sheepish look. With this look, he would surely inherit the earth.

Then, across the room, I was sure I spotted the tall woman with the caper eyes. I jumped up, and I searched frantically for others: the girl with the mouth and her mother, Zoli, Mary, Mrs. Molnar, Andras and Gisela, in case they were leaving from here, and Father Tamas— where was he going? On what rock was he going to build his new church? I was always expecting something, look- ing for someone familiar. I did see the blond girl with the green-checked dress—she was peering back our way in the distance—but that was all. I wasn't sure if I should wave and decided not to.

I was on the verge of salting up when Attila noticed someone, a boy, taller, bigger, and darker than Attila was, pass by our row of cots. "Look!" Attila said, jumping up. "He was on the swim team that beat us in the relays, from Saint Hilda's School, over in the eighth district, and they beat us in water polo too, and in both they cheated their heads off. They pulled little tricks under the surface and brought in a ringer. What's his name?" Attila was punching his own side.

"I don't know," I said.

"What's his goddamn name?" Attila punched the air and even jumped once. The boy was some distance away now. "Hey," Attila yelled, and the boy turned. "Hey!"

The boy came over and looked down at my excited brother's sunny hair. Clearly, he could not make out who my brother was, let alone name him.

"You!" my brother barked.

"What?" the boy said, except he was really a man in every respect but age.

"You don't know my name," my idiot brother said as he poked the man-boy in the chest. "You don't know who I am, do you?"

"Do you know my name?" the boy said, poking Attila all the way back down into a sitting position on his cot.

Attila leapt up into the boy's face. "Do you know what?" He poked him again. "You don't forget my name. I forget yours. You got that?"

The boy tried to push my brother back down, but Attila stood firm and glared up into his opponent's face. Our father was now standing too, but the boy moved off.

Within ninety seconds of this incident, my brother was asleep.

Our grandmother and parents filed by to kiss us, and the lights soon went out. I didn't want to disturb anyone or trip over anything searching for a window, so I stayed put in the darkness, but I wished there'd been a window, like the one in the convent.

I don't know how long I waited, but I heard someone whispering in a cot not far away, and then I heard the sound of kissing and cooing. I lifted my head off the pillow, strained in the darkness to see the sloshy, gaspy couple, but couldn't make out a thing. If creamy pastries made a sound, this was it. I tried to imagine what the pair looked like, how old they were, how they managed on these little cots, but in the end I didn't want to know. I would add the incident to my bank of secrets.

TEN

THAT NIGHT AS WE were boarding the bus marked PARIS, an Austrian police officer and a man in a black trench coat who was holding a notebook detained our father. My father urged us to get on and take our seats, but Attila wouldn't hear of it. He leered at the men and looked ready to lunge. Our grandmother and mother had to stand in his way.

Luckily, our father was soon released. He was shaking his head and had a furious look on his face when he joined us.

"What did they want?" Attila said.

"Not now," our mother said.

"They wanted to know about Paul," our father said.

"*Our* Paul? Paul *Beck?*" she asked.

"Yes, Paul Beck."

"Our cousin?" my brother said.

"What did you tell them?" our grandmother asked.

"I told them what I know—nothing."

"We do know nothing," our mother said.

"That's what I told them."

"Were they both Austrian?" our grandmother asked.

"No, only the policeman. The other one might have been an agent of some kind, a French government agent."

Our grandmother looked pale. I knew right away that the conversation was over.

The bus driver wanted us to take our seats. He spoke to us in French but was not friendly. My mother shot him numerous unanswered smiles just to cheer him up, and I shot him several lesser ones, but the man was all grim business. He glanced at our papers. These, naturally, didn't excite him either. He was keen to get going.

"What about Paul?" Attila said again as we worked our way to the back.

"Nothing," our father said.

"What *about* him?" my brother insisted.

"You know as much about him as I do. Now be quiet." My father looked fierce, which only sometimes made my brother back down, but this time it worked.

It was my turn. "Was Paul your first cousin?" I asked our father.

"Yes," he said more kindly. "His father, Heinrich, and my father were brothers."

The bus was full, and here the seats did not face each other. We were all arranged in pairs facing forward, the usual way. Attila and I had quite a wrestling match over the window seat, but our mother stepped in and sat with Attila so he could have a window. Our grandmother sat with me across the aisle so I could too. Our father sat next to a man with an impressive mustache, which had sharp ends and looked like a propeller blade. The man had been a lawyer and judge, he said, and was meeting his nephew in Paris to plan his next move.

We were visiting our great-aunt Hermina, the famous opera singer, our father told the man, who said he knew about her.

"She's quite a singer," the man said, "but she has not been back in Hungary for some time."

"No," our father said. "She's been living in Paris for years now."

"Naturally," the man said, but I didn't know what he meant.

I got out my Pez Tin Man and popped a candy from its neck. My grandmother didn't want one. I worried suddenly about the marzipan monkey in my bag and hoped he had made the long journey without getting deformed.

We drove quite a long way before Attila leaned over our mother across the seats to tell me that we were meeting the Crow Woman.

Both women jumped in. Our mother said, "Don't speak about your grandmother's sister in that way."

Our grandmother balled her hands into fists.

"But it's true," Attila said, and he held up his fingers like claws. "Her hands are like a crow's talons. She can't straighten her fingers." He was still making his claws, raking the air and, for some reason, hissing like a tiger.

"Is that true, Mamu?" I asked.

My grandmother said her sister had suffered a trauma in the war and was not to be mocked. "Why would you add to her misfortune by making fun of her?" she asked us both.

"What happened to her?" I asked.

"Ask *them,*" my brother said.

"Attila, please," said our mother.

My brother lunged at her. "I feel we have a right to know, now that we are men, or at least I am. You said you'd tell me what happened once I was ready to hear about it."

Our father, in his seat in front of us, turned his head. "You'll never be ready," he said.

"Simon, why must you say such things about your bright sons?"

"They're not that bright."

"They're very bright."

"Brightness is not the point, in any case," he said. "You know what I'm saying."

"I don't know what you're saying," I said. I turned to our grandmother. "Why can't we know?"

"News like that can wait. Trust me, my angel."

"But I can't wait," Attila said.

"You will wait," our grandmother said. "And don't make fun of your great-aunt, especially since you know she suffered. Hermina doesn't like people to know about it. She has a right to keep these matters to herself."

"Mother," my brother said, "I need your help."

"Not this time," she said. She was not smiling, and

because my mother's smile was so true and natural, its disappearance was like the end of happiness.

Attila huffed and turned toward his window.

I felt sick now. What had happened to our cousin Paul? What had happened to our great-aunt Hermina? Why had so many members of our family been marked in this way, made to suffer? And those were the lucky ones, the ones who'd made it. At that moment, I could not look out my window at my half of the world the way Attila was looking at his half. If my window had served up the Eiffel Tower or plopped down a pyramid, I could not have cared.

My brother had met Hermina just once, when she came back to Budapest to sing, and I had known her only through glamorous photographs, especially one that showed her dressed as Emperor Nero's bride, Poppea. She stood with Nero on the cover of a Hungarian national opera program. Attila had seen that opera with our grandmother, but I hadn't. She had worried that I was too young.

I said to my grandmother, "Does Aunt Hermina still sing?"

"Oh, yes, she sings," Mamu said. "She might even sing for you. She loves baroque. Maybe she'll sing some Handel or Bach. Do you remember the songs the nuns were singing?" I nodded yes. "Those were baroque too."

I told my grandmother about the Statue Graveyard, which Attila had taken me to. She had never seen it.

"We saw the Swedish man there, at the graveyard. We saw Raoul Wallenberg."

"What?" she asked. Our mother had heard me too, as had our father and the man with the propeller mustache. Attila seemed the least interested in what I was saying.

"I don't mean the man. I mean the monument."

"Oh." My grandmother put a hand on her heart. My mother smiled.

I wanted to know, specifically, what Raoul Wallenberg had done for us.

"Quite a bit," my grandmother said. "We wouldn't be on this bus if not for him."

"And my cousin Paul," our father said.

"Not now," said our grandmother.

"Tell us about Paul," Attila said right away.

"He's—" our father began.

"Not now!" our grandmother insisted and stamped her foot.

Even Attila backed off. "Then when?" he asked.

"Your poor grandfather would not have wanted you ever to know."

"Robert?" I said.

"Yes, my Robert. Dear Robert." She sighed. "Another time," she said. "I promise."

A while later, our mother took Attila and me to the water closet in the back of the bus, and when we returned to our seats, Attila put his head down on our mother's lap and went straight to sleep. I wondered if the statue of Mor Jokai would still be allowed to guard our street back home and how long he would last. Would he outlast the street? Would the time come for him to take a seat at the Statue Graveyard, watch over it for a while?

I strained to hear love sounds as I had back in the dormitory in Vienna, but the bus's motor was too loud, even if there were any.

Except for our driver and me, everyone on the bus was having quite a snooze, sitting straight up or lying on someone's lap or leaning against a rattling window. The driver himself must have been fighting off sleep.

The moon was full and outlined the shape of things, like a night artist. I wondered why the moon had to be round. What if it were square, to line up with windows? It would be like a Picasso painting I'd seen at the National Gallery—a painting of lovers, all their features pulled to the front, sitting under the bright glowing square. The only risk I could see was that if the moon were square it might mock the sun rather than doing the important job of reflecting its light.

ELEVEN

WE WERE ALL ROUSED by a jolt. A shoe and a bag fell off the rack above our heads, and a bottle rolled toward the front and shattered on something. My tired eyes struggled to interpret the vinegary dawn. "France," I heard a couple of people on the bus say.

My father and the man with the propeller mustache looked coldly at each other, like the strangers they were. My mother had ripe pears in her bag, and she offered one to each of us, including the propeller man, but he declined. The bus kept rolling into the thin light.

France.

The countryside seemed too bashful to be France, the land of Napoleon and Louis XIV and the Three Musketeers. There wasn't much to it: some rocks and fields, a bridge over a creek, some wooden houses with small vineyards out back, a weak sun.

My pear was juicy and sweet. I finished first, before Attila, and he knew it, but he acted as if he didn't notice. He hung his hands over the seat in front, our father's seat, and said to him, "Can I hear now about Raoul Wallenberg and Paul Beck?"

Our father didn't answer him. Our mother and grandmother looked straight ahead.

"The war was over in Hungary," Attila said. "Can you at least tell me why the Russians took Raoul Wallenberg?"

The man with the propeller mustache, the former judge, half turned in his seat and said, "The Russians removed Wallenberg because he was a menace."

"What did you say?" our father asked. He was grinding his teeth.

"The Swede was an interloper. He had no business in Hungary."

"He was saving Hungarians."

"Not exactly," the man said.

Attila stood up, hovering over the men from behind.

"You know Wallenberg was trying to impede the Germans' removal of people of impure blood," the man continued. "Cosmopolitans. Gypsies. Jews. Swedes, or *manufactured* Swedes, I should say."

"The Germans were removing Hungarian nationals," our father said. "I am a Hungarian national, an expatriate, a refugee. As are you. As are we all on this bus."

"That's a matter of opinion," the man said, and he looked straight ahead rather than at my father.

My brother was leaning over the seat, huffing right

into the man's hair. Our mother reached over to put a hand on our father's shoulder. She had a pleading look that said, "Enough. Please, leave it alone."

But my father couldn't. "Did you say you were a judge?" he asked.

The man turned back toward him. He too was huffing. Others on the bus could hear the commotion now.

"By not finishing their work," the man said, "the Germans have unleashed a species twice as noxious as the original. Survivors who have been wronged. Righteous whiners. Seekers of justice all over the planet. Hounding the rest of us to an early grave. Wanting—nay, *needing*—to make us repent. I knew it would happen. I knew it instantly."

The man got to his feet.

Our father did as well and moved out into the aisle, where the man joined him. "By 'the rest of us,'" our father said, "do you mean those of pure blood?"

"That's exactly what I mean. Your impure blood. It's the very thing you're going to export now to foreign lands. With your impure selves. Your righteousness. Your victimhood. It's what we'll hear until the end of time. Prattle, prattle, prattle, until we're ready to do anything, give you anything, just to make you shut up." As he spoke, the man made a prattling mouth out of his hand and flapped it in our father's face. "Everyone will go on hating Jews. You might succeed in driving the hatred underground. People will appear to like you. People will act as though they want to side with what is right and just. But even the people who appear to like you won't.

Not really. And they'll look for the first excuse to let you know it."

Attila lunged at the propeller man's neck, nearly knocking over our mother, but our father stood in his way and shoved him back down.

"Do you see what I mean?" the man said. "Cage your hellcat."

Our father grabbed the judge by the collar and lifted him until the man's feet left the floor of the bus. A woman called out—screamed, actually. It was the woman with the dangly pearl earrings and matching necklace. I hadn't seen her board this bus too. The driver slowed the vehicle and shouted something over his shoulder at our father. He even blasted his horn twice.

Our father let the judge down. The man had a smirk on his face. His propeller mustache was as crisp as ever, its blades turned up. "Just as I predicted," he said. "Ha!"

Out of nowhere, as if it had been a concealed weapon, my father's fist shot up, a Superman fist, straight into the man's chin. There was a terrible clack, and then the jaw unhinged and the man fell backwards to the floor with a thud. The woman in pearls cried out again. Blood spread from the side of the judge's mouth. The bus swerved to the side of the road.

The woman with the pearls tended to the man.

"Is he dead?" my brother asked.

The woman shook her head. She bent down to feel the man's breath, hear his chest.

"What did you do?" our mother said.

"I shut him up," our father said.

The driver came back toward us.

"Drive!" our father said in Hungarian. "Drive!" He held up his fist. "Paris!" he added with a French accent. The word, the way he said it, didn't seem to go with the fist.

The driver stopped, turned, and timidly returned to his seat.

Our father was still standing over the fallen man when he said to Attila, "Now, what was it you wanted to know?"

"Simon!" our mother shouted. "Sit down. We're in enough trouble."

Our father was still huffy. I could almost see his heart pounding through his shirt.

"We're not in any kind of trouble," he said, half out of breath.

"This man won't complain for some time," the woman with the pearls said. She was tying up the judge's jaw with a scarf. The man moaned but stayed put.

The mood of the whole bus had changed. My brother and I were both sitting in the aisle seats now, right across from each other. My grandmother gripped my hand. Attila looked hot and pink.

Our father was sitting again, saying nothing, staring out into the gray morning.

"Aren't we Hungarian?" I asked my brother.

"We're not anything."

"Aren't we Hungarian until we become something else? What did the man mean?"

"Dad should have finished the bastard off. I would

have stepped on his neck, ground it, and crushed it into powder."

Our mother shook her head. She and our grand-mother still seemed shaken.

I joined our father, and he took my hand and moved over to where the judge had sat, by the window. We both spent a long while staring at the silver sun, the impostor sun.

When we got to Paris late in the morning, Attila helped our father carry the man out. They laid him down on a bench. Our father stared the driver down, and the man loped away. He busied himself with whatever luggage the passengers had stored.

Our father checked on the judge again, still lying on the bench, with his eyes open. One of his propeller blades was turned downward now. It gave the man half a frown. He looked alarmed when our father asked him how he felt, and he reached up to feel his jaw. Then he waved our father away. When our grandmother tried, he waved her away too.

"Go," he was telling all of us with a violent wave. "Go."

TWELVE

WE TOOK A TAXI from the bus station to the 16th arrondissement, as our grandmother called it. The streets looked like sculpture gardens to me—the buildings and bridges and even the subway and bus stops. It was like driving through an outdoor art gallery.

The driver wanted to be paid in advance and would not accept Hungarian currency, no matter how much we offered, so our grandmother gave him her pinkie ring with the turquoise stone. She said she didn't like it much anyway, but I'd never seen her without it on.

When we pulled up in front of Aunt Hermina's home, the music coming from it was so loud that the whole street rumbled under our wheels. It was as if an entire opera house had been squeezed into our great-aunt's white town house. We had to ring the doorbell repeatedly. No one answered until there was a lull in the aria.

Then the door opened, and there stood Hermina, every bit as glamorous as Nero's Poppea about to receive the crown. She was a thinner, younger, taller version of her sister, our grandmother. Our grandmother was the eldest in her family, and Hermina was the youngest, but I could easily tell that they were sisters. Our great-aunt had the same caramel eyes, the same auburn hair, except that hers was highlighted with strands of gold and whipped up onto her head in weaves and folds.

The aria started up again, and the music was gigantic, big as a canyon.

Our father pushed past his aunt, shouting, "You're disturbing the peace!"

"Darling," Hermina said, "Handel is incapable of disturbing the peace."

Our father went searching for the phonograph and switched it off.

As we stood in the ripe quiet, Aunt Hermina hummed the last notes of the aria. "Did you like what you heard, my darling?" she asked my brother.

"If you like a lightning bolt to the ear," he said.

"*Toujours* Attila," Hermina said.

"Where is Andras?" she asked. "Where's Judit? You wired that you were all coming together."

Our grandmother took her sister's face in her hands and told her what had become of Judit and Andras and little Gisela. The sisters looked at each other, then put their foreheads together. Our mother joined them, and the three swayed together but said nothing more.

I was going to join the huddle with the women but

wanted to see what our father and Attila would do first. They stayed where they stood, and both hung their heads, so I hung my head too. I gulped repeatedly as I imagined little Gisela.

It seemed like a very long time before my brother said, "Our father beat up a man on the bus."

"He did what?" Hermina asked, pulling away from the other women.

"Please, darling, let's not talk about it just yet," our grandmother said as she kissed her sister.

We left our bags and stepped into Hermina's salon, which was like stepping into a French pastry, all billowy with creams and pallors, marzipan and peach. There was nothing crisp about the place. It was all soft lines and colors. An ivory grand piano sat poised in a tall bay window like an albino alligator with its jaw open wide. A portrait in oil of Hermina in her young years, her warm eyes gazing out over the room, hung above a plush blond sofa. On the opposite wall was a painting of a summerhouse with two children standing on the grass out front. The children had no faces. "It's called *Garden with Trees*," Hermina told me as I studied the picture. "Do you like it?"

I nodded. I did like it, though I didn't know how I would fill in the faces.

Hermina herself was dressed in a cream floral gown that went with the room, and she wore blush-pink gloves. She smoothed my hair at the back with a warm hand. "My little dark beauty," she said in a honeyed voice. Now she cupped my face in the bowl of her gloved hands. "So this is the one," she said, looking at her sister.

133

What about the golden beauty, I wanted to know? What about Attila? "My dark beauty," she said again as she raised my face to the light and kissed me straight on the lips. A charge shot down my spine to my tail. She kissed my brother in the same way, but she was moving on, directing all movement in the room, inviting everyone to sit, get comfortable. Her housekeeper, Babette, brought in a tray heavy with croissants, petits fours and apricot preserves, tea, coffee, and cocoa specially made for my brother and me. Our parents and grandmother asked for a few minutes to sort out our things and left the room.

Babette was young and blond and brown-eyed. She smiled radiantly. I could easily see a smiling duel lining up between Babette and our mother. She reminded me a bit of Sister Heidi, but Babette did not hide her beauty in the way of nuns. She lingered an extra moment and fluffed up a cushion as my brother and I gawked at her.

Attila and I shared a large ottoman, where we ate and drank heartily as our great-aunt watched us. She was childless and a widow now. Our grandmother had told us that Uncle Ede and Aunt Hermina had moved to this house when he was invited to teach medicine at the university. He had just retired from his post when he died quietly one morning behind his newspaper.

"You never had children," my brother said.

"No," said Hermina.

"You couldn't?"

"We could, I think."

"So why didn't you?" Attila asked. I'm not sure our mother and grandmother would have let this question fly.

Hermina sighed. "I would have been a bad mother," she said. "I would have been a bad mother even if I'd given birth to myself." She chuckled, but we both stared at her in horror. She looked away.

My brother took a bite of pastry, nudged me with his elbow, and pointed with his face at Hermina's hands, wanting me to take note of the claws. "Aunt Hermina," he said, "what happened to your hands?"

"Can we save our dark tales for a dark afternoon," she said gently, "when we're locked up in here?"

Attila finished what was in his mouth and said, "I saw you in the opera in Budapest."

"I know, darling. I knew you were there. I was very glad. Did you like the opera? It was Monteverdi's master-piece, *L'incoronazione di Poppea. The Coronation of Poppea.*"

"I liked one song," Attila said. He licked jam from the corner of his mouth.

"Just one?" she asked. She laughed.

"Yes, and I've been meaning to ask you a series of questions ever since."

"A *series?*" she said and laughed again. "Let's see if we have answers this time." She sat up in her white chair and clasped her gloved hands together in her lap.

"I thought I was going to die a slow, writhing death," Attila said. Aunt Hermina sat as still as her painted self. "The opera was endless," he went on. "Until that last song. When stupid Nero is crowning his Poppea, his second wife, I guess."

Aunt Hermina's warm eyes widened. I looked at her lips, the ones that had kissed mine.

"For me," Attila said, "it was the first true moment, the first one that didn't feel fake."

"Fake?"

"It was hard to believe you could love that big fat Nero, but then suddenly I did believe it because Nero was giving you a crown to prove his love. Until then, he thought too much, and he sang out every boring thought, but really talk-singing rather than just talking."

"And then there was the song," Aunt Hermina said eagerly.

"Yes, then came that song. For me, it was the one single real moment, as I said. The two of you sang 'Pur ti miro.' Mamu helped me later with the words."

This was the song the Gypsy beggar had hummed back in Budapest!

Attila closed his eyes dramatically. He put his hand on his heart. "'I adore you,' Poppea is saying, and he is saying it back. 'I hold you. I want you. I *enchain* you.'"

"But, darling," Hermina said. "Remember, he is crowning her. There is irony there."

Attila opened his eyes. "Irony? Not in the song," my brother said. "The song is about real love. It didn't even match the songs that went before it. It was like someone else had dreamed it up and written it."

"Maybe it was another composer," Aunt Hermina said good-naturedly.

"Yes," Attila said. He jumped up off the ottoman. "What if it was? Claudio Monteverdi had students. It was someone young, a young man, probably, and he was studying with the master, and maybe one day the student

presented the master with a little tune he had composed, a song inspired, maybe, by the master himself. He
wanted the master to approve of his work. He might have
said to the composer, 'It's called "Pur ti miro."' Claudio looks over the pages of music. He looks up at the
boy, who is not wearing a wig the way the master is.
Claudio knows what he is holding. He says to his pupil,
'Let me think about it. I'll look it over again. Let me
just give it a second look.' And he rubs his chin, most
likely, almost certainly, and pulls on his sharp beard for
effect. The pupil grins and bows and raises his hands as
if in prayer to his own god, the composer, the father of
opera, and backs out of the room, tiptoes out, and never
comes back. Somehow, he disappears. Just like that." Attila snapped his fingers. "He never comes back to find
out what's happened to his song. But his song doesn't disappear. Not his lovely song. His song moves to the top of
the opera. And it stays there at the finale. Waiting for the
night you sang it for me."

"Sometimes these things drop from heaven, quite by
accident," Hermina said. "Sometimes an angel comes
through the window and sits by the composer until he
has his song."

"Yes, but which composer did the angel visit? And did
the angel visit one composer while the devil visited the
other?"

Our great-aunt was staring at my brother. "What an
imagination you have, you dear boy," she said. "But let
me ask you. What if Monteverdi did compose 'Pur ti
miro'? Why would you take it away from him?"

"It doesn't fit—for me, I mean. That's all. So I'm just saying."

"It doesn't matter, dear. What matters is that we have the song. Can't we just be happy for the song?"

Attila moved close to our great-aunt. She was pinned to her seat. "But it bothers me," he said.

"What does?"

"Truth. Doesn't truth matter?"

"The kind of truth you're looking for relies more on a feeling, a hunch, rather than on proof," she said. "A hunch lives in the world of instinct and belief, not proof. You loved the song, my darling. Love is its own truth. Isn't it?"

Attila considered the point. He looked at Hermina without responding.

"In the end, my dear, the person hardly matters. No one knows where Mozart is buried, but we have his music." She looked down at her gloved hands.

My brother sat back down again beside me. He was glowing like a glowhead.

Hermina stroked the column of her neck with her gloved hand. I thought she might have been blushing. "What an imagination you have, my dear," she said again. "Do angels visit you?"

"Angels and devils," my brother said, very satisfied with himself.

I ate a plump chocolate. It was molten sweet. It flowed brownly down my throat.

Our great-aunt reached for a mother-of-pearl box beside her on the table. An ivory swan perched on its lid.

She opened the box and released the music trapped inside. "It's *Swan Lake,*" she said. It was a snuffbox. Using a snuff spoon, she lifted some to her nose and breathed in. "Snuff?" she said to us.

"Sure," said my brother. He took a wad in his fingers and snorted it hard, all the way up into his brain.

The inquiries didn't end there. Over a glittering dinner in a dining room with windows as tall as masts, our father asked Hermina why she was staying in Paris still.

We were having veal goulash with dumplings, to remind us of home. Babette had served it from a porcelain tureen. She'd smiled at each of us as she did so. My brother and I followed her every move. Babette knew we were admiring her but didn't break her stride. When she set down the tureen between us and stepped back, my brother whispered to me, "If only I had the gift of that Noseboy on the bus, just to interpret these joyous scents." Babette was blushing as if she knew what we were saying. The pink suited her blond face. Attila and I kept staring, but she withdrew, aiming her warm blush away from us.

"Why don't you leave with us?" our father said. "It seems like the best plan, considering."

Hermina chewed and chewed and chewed while we watched and waited for her mouth to come to a stop.

Finally, she said, "I can't start again somewhere else. My Ede and I started again here. This, for me, is as good as it gets. My Ede is buried here, in Passy. I visit him and chat with him. Sometimes, if I have more to say to him than usual, I set a place for him at this table. I go to con-

139

certs and galleries and museums. I sing here and watch others sing and dance. I love the culture. Everything I need and want is here."

"Yes, culture," our father said.

"Yes, *culture,*" Hermina repeated, turning up the heat in her voice.

"You're like my mother. You believe culture is restricted to a few special places."

"Thank you for the compliment," Mamu said.

"No, not restricted," Hermina said. "But it doesn't spring up just anywhere like a mushroom. It takes centuries to cultivate. You are going where? The New World, New York, *Canada?* I sang in Canada once, in Montreal. What is the formula there in Canada—draw everyone together into a huddle and then refrigerate? It's a place to start. A nice, clean, fresh place, to be sure, but a place to start only. I still have hope for Europe, for France."

Our father took quite a scoop of dumplings into his mouth. He was a fast eater at the best of times, but now he wanted to add drama, so he chewed and chewed and chewed the way Hermina had. Finally, he said, "So we are the cultivated ones on this side of the planet—the supremely cultivated."

Hermina set down her mighty fork and knife. She was at the head of the table, looking queenly in a powder-green evening gown with her hair up. "In a word, yes, some of us are," she said. "It's never all of us. But it takes centuries to grow a Handel or a Beethoven. Millennia, even. Think of the achievements of Europeans, of Europe."

"Achievement is overrated. We're on the run from it. One day you're living in a golden tower, the next it topples."

My grandmother was about to say something, but her sister held up her hand. "It's all right, Klari," she said, taking a breath but looking hard at my father. My mother aimed the same look at him. Attila was smiling through a full mouth. "Do you think Handel and Beethoven and Goethe are overrated?" Hermina asked.

My father did not put down his cutlery. That would have been going too far. "Yes," he said. "The Germans were the most cultivated people on earth, weren't they, the highest achievers?"

No one spoke. Attila's cheek was bulging with food, and he bobbed back and forth in his chair. His eyes, alive with questions, glittered in the lights of the room.

"The most cultivated culture we have ever known, the Germans," my father continued. "Tell us what happened to you there, in the land of Handel?"

"Simon," Mamu said, "why are you tormenting my sister? Why do the Beck boys always torment her?"

I was innocent, but my face burned anyway.

"Please," Hermina said. She again held up her gloved hand, forest green on this occasion. "I haven't had such lively conversation around this table since my Ede took his leave. I'm glad to have the dazzling Beck boys with me and, of course, the Beck girls." She turned back to her nephew. "I'm not moving to Germany either, my dear," she said. "But the Germans are going through their cycle of self-hatred after loving themselves too much,

141

after needing to hate others to sustain their delusion. Hubris. It does in whole nations, whole empires."

"Hubris. Is that all it was?"

Hermina shrugged.

"Yet Germany remains with us," our father said. "You love your Handel, do you not?"

Our mother rolled her eyes.

"Handel belongs to all of humanity," Hermina said, "not just Germany."

"The same culture produced both," my father said. "You can't have one without the other. You can't have Handel without Hitler."

"You're making my point for me," she answered. "You need that darkness—a few drops of darkness—to brighten the light. Handel's beauty has a darkness at its core, a sweet, incurable sadness." We were all staring at our great-aunt. "That was his secret," she said. "But we all have secrets, don't we?" She looked first at our father, then at the two other adults, stopping at her sister.

"Please, Hermi," our grandmother said.

"I once had white, supple hands, and now they are forever clothed." She made fists and held them up to the chandelier. "I can still pack a punch, though," she said, and then turned to Attila and me. "What is your secret, boys?"

I blushed hotly, though there was no secret I could think of that I had been hiding.

"What about it, Simon?" Even our father blushed. "Lili? Klari?"

"You're tormenting us now," Mamu said. "What is the matter with this family?"

142

"We all have our shameful deeds to forget."

"And what shameful deed might that be in our case?" our father said. "To make it through one war to welcome the next one? Is that our evil deed? Fleeing a hostile country? Is that our evil deed?"

"I didn't say evil."

"Shameful, then."

"Have you heard from Paul lately?" she asked.

"Hermina!" Mamu said, slapping the table and getting up from it.

Our father said, "I'm not sure what our crime was or our secret, Aunt Hermina."

"You mean Paul Beck?" Attila said to our great-aunt.

"Yes, Paul Beck," Hermina said. "You could have stopped it, all of you." She looked at my parents, my grandmother. "You *should* have stopped it. But everyone stood by."

"Stopped *what?*" Attila asked.

"Enough," Mamu said. "Thank you, Hermi, truly."

Everyone was getting up, except me.

"What could we have stopped?" Attila said.

Hermina had a smirk on her face I hadn't seen earlier, as dark as I imagined Handel's was, maybe darker.

I stayed for a dessert of chestnut puree with whipped cream—Attila too, but just for a few seconds. He scarfed his down, so I was alone at the table when Babette brought me cocoa. She smiled as if there was nothing amiss in the festive dining room. She seemed to be admiring me, and I admired her back. Everything smelled of cream—warm cream. And also chestnuts.

THIRTEEN

Attila and I were to sleep in the library. We each had a daybed right underneath bulging bookcases mounted on the wall.

"What were they talking about?" I asked my brother.

"I'm not sure, but we're going to find out. Give me a day, my ever-curious darling."

Hermina came in to see that we were settled. "I have something for each of you," she said. She was holding a leather-covered slipcase with two books tucked into it. "I picked them out especially for you. Your first books in English. We can read them together, if you want to try. I don't speak English the way Paul did, but I do speak some, and read some." She pulled the first book out. "They're both by Mark Twain, a writer who lived in the New World, where you're headed." She gave it to my brother. It was *The Adventures of Tom Sawyer*.

She then gave me mine, and I tried to sound out the title: "*Da Udventoors of Hoockleberry Feenn.*"

Our great-aunt smiled at me and kissed me on the forehead.

She was followed by our grandmother, who did the same, but on this night our mother didn't come in. Mamu said she might later. I could hear her in a nearby room talking heatedly with our father.

I wondered who would get to keep the nice leather case for the two books. Wouldn't the books have to stay together when they weren't being read?

Once we switched off the lights I could think of nothing but the wall of books above me, the voices sealed in the pages, the heft of the books. What would happen if each book were given its own room, like the room it was written in? What a palace you'd need to house them all! I strained to hear my brother's breathing, but he was as quiet as could be. Attila was such a warrior that I was surprised that he could give himself up to anything so abruptly.

Then I heard the sound of running water and someone humming, a woman, but very faint. I crept out of the library. At the far end of a dark corridor, a crack of light shone against the wall. I moved toward it as quietly as I could. The carpet was prickly and warm beneath my bare feet. As I got closer to the light, the humming grew louder. My heart seemed to be in a marching band but could not keep its beat. The floor creaked once, but the water and the humming continued, so I did too. When I got to the door the sliver of light was coming from, I held my breath as I peered in. What I saw could have cured blindness.

Babette was inside. She was drawing a bath. She barely looked real to me. Her form was soft and white. She could have been a sylph living in a myth or a fairy tale. Her robe slipped off her shoulders. I was not sure I was breathing, but my timpani heart took all the hungry air it needed. I wanted to flee or to faint, but I could not move. And then Babette looked over her white shoulder and saw me. She didn't gasp, didn't hide herself or even turn away but smiled her creamy smile. I was the one who gasped, who ducked into the shadows and dashed back to my room with a terrible racket.

I found my bed below the bookcase and tucked myself into it. I tried to catch a deep breath, but my heart kept pounding for several more minutes, expecting something, hoping Babette might visit, but possibly not, better not.

It started to rain, quietly at first, but then harder, louder. It rained tables and chairs, but strangely there was no thunder or lightning. It felt warm and dry in this bed in our great-aunt's town house in Paris. I found myself hoping the man we'd left on the bench at the bus station had made it inside.

That first night in Paris, I dreamt about Gerbeaud. I was alone and walking through rain, but I could see Gerbeaud ahead through the wet light. I rushed toward it, skidding sometimes on the cobblestones of Vorosmarty Square.

But then a single skid winged me all the way to the banks of the Danube, where all of the bridges had fallen, even the Liberty, even the Chain Bridge! Only its central pillar punched itself out of the water. What had the Russians done? Or was it the Germans, the Ottomans, the Avars, the hordes? The destruction looked bigger, even, than war. It looked biblical. It looked like a decree: I will smite you down. I will divide Buda from Pest, ever to remain so.

Small boats chugged between Buda and Pest. On the other side, wings of buildings were down, if the buildings stayed standing at all. The Hotel Gellert's grand entrance had sagged into its thermal baths below. The mighty flag-pole that stood on its high base in front of the National Gallery flew no flag, though I could still see the great bronze eagle perched on its stone mount, getting set to take flight, always poised in this same way but never managing to lift itself up. A row of elegant white town houses had fallen forward down the slope of the green hill, like backbones cut from their caps and tails.

I stood in the drizzle and thought I spotted my friend Zoli on the other side. I tried to call out to him, but I had lost my voice to the dampness. Where was he headed? He lived on this side, in Pest. Who was he running from?

A single motorboat throbbed in its slip below me. The riverbank under my feet trembled. I turned toward Gresham Palace, one of its shoulders damaged by a bomb. Russian soldiers floated in and out of its grand doors and windows—but not fluttering, strictly floating. These were not fluttering things. I had to get back to Café Gerbeaud. I went the long way, around Gresham Palace.

148

My heart flapped in its cage. I took off at full speed as if I were being chased.

I could not see the banner of Papa Stalin draped down over Kossuth's department store. The store was gone, the building, even the corner it stood on. But up ahead, the beacon of Gerbeaud still stood, waiting for my return. It was guarded by a Russian soldier, the *same* soldier with the bushel of beard who'd given me the *matryoshka* doll. He glanced at me as if he'd been expecting me and waved me on. But there was no one else entering Gerbeaud or leaving it, no one in sight, and it was dark inside — in the middle of the afternoon.

I moved close to the window, lifted my hand to shelter my eyes from the rain. The monkey's golden cage still gleamed in the center of the café, even with the lights out, but the cage was empty. The generous glass cases, which had contained the cakes and chocolates and marzipan figures, were empty. Not a crumb remained.

The kitchen door opened, and a rectangle of light imprinted itself on the room. There was a man back there, a baker dressed all in white, and he was talking to someone. He spotted me. I could smell baking. The aroma reached me like a warm hand. I scooted around to the side of the building.

The door opened, and at first I saw no one, until I felt a tapping on my knee and looked down at the monkey. He was not wearing his bellman's cap and vest, but he showed me the way in, like a doorman. I was thrilled.

The baker beckoned. "Please," he said, and he offered me a wooden kitchen chair. He was baking, had taken out a few loaves of golden braided egg bread from the oven.

"You're still here," I said. "And the kaiser."

"We were lucky to get him back."

I asked where he'd been. I felt steam rising from my back in this warm kitchen.

The baker whispered to me that Tarzan had taken the kaiser to his home in the jungle. Tarzan had wailed and the kaiser had wailed, and the man had called him Cheetah, but Cheetah could not swing through the trees like the man. He strained himself and hurt his hand on the jagged vines.

The kaiser reached for the baker's hand. He'd heard this story before. Maybe it was the whisper that gave it away. The baker's mustache was the exact same oak brown as the kaiser's fur, and he and the monkey both had the same brown downturned eyes, like clowns' eyes. The monkey was patting the baker's hand and urging him on.

The baker said that it was then, after Cheetah fell to the forest floor, that a golden-haired beauty called Babette came out of the warm water, kissed his fingers, and made them well.

As if on cue, the monkey held up the healed fingers. I held them and looked them over.

The baker said that the kaiser had then found his way back to Gerbeaud, though it took some stealth on his part.

I compared the monkey to a cat and patted him on the head. The kaiser stood up, squealed, and leapt onto the baker's board. He selected one of the loaves of egg bread and broke off a piece to offer to me. The baker asked me to accept it so as not to offend the kaiser. Of course I did. The kaiser tore off a good piece for himself too, bowed, and sat back down. I marveled at his opposable thumbs. Attila was big on opposable thumbs, often commending the Lord and Nature for coming up with them. I tasted the morsel, the warm goodness of it, the egg, the flour, the milk, fresh from the farms in the countryside around Budapest.

The baker said that it was the only thing the Russians allowed him to bake now. "No sweets. Only necessities, not luxuries. Bread is food," he told me. "Dessert is a luxury. But I am mad with baking. I imagine painting the ceiling of the Sistine Chapel, and they give me the inside of a hat to paint instead. They're even going to change the name of the place. *Gerbeaud* is too pretty, they said, too frivolous."

I asked if they were going to call it Kaiser Laszlo. I was still chewing.

The man shook his head. He told me there was to be no kaiser there, no heads of state. He smiled at the monkey. "The Russians do love this kaiser as much as anything," he said, "and he obliges. They pet him, and he pets them. It is the end of the Kingdom of Sugar, the Palace of Chocolates, the Royal Grove of Nut Trees— almonds, walnuts, hazelnuts, chestnuts—the fall of the Palace of Excess."

I finally finished what was in my mouth.

Maybe the next time the kaiser returned to the woods,

he could open his own place, treat his former friends to a little café life. He could bake tarts and breads for them, ask them to gather berries and nuts for his creations. After all, how many monkeys in the world had thought to have desserts? It would easily make him kaiser to monkeys large and small, as he had been to women and men, boys and girls. What I mean is, was there ever any going back to the woods for Laszlo?

What I mean, number two, is that it is desserts that set us apart. How many other species eat dessert?

The kaiser stretched himself out on the baker's board. I patted his shoulder, but he moved my hand to his chest, his heart. The place was soft with fur, but most of all it was warm. Something happened, a current ran up through my arm like a rising sound, coming from a distant place, the notes of a long-gone composer, calling from a cave out into the light. I lifted out of the chair, floated up, and gazed back down at my hand on the furry heart beating under my palm like an unborn child.

My hand burned. My own heart yammered. I landed again and yanked my hand back. I stood up out of the lean chair. The kaiser stood too, on the baking board, and threw his arms around my neck.

"I have to go," I said over his arm to the baker.

With some difficulty, the baker took down the clinging monkey.

"I'll come back, though," I said. "I'll be back."

★ ★ ★

I looked up through the Paris darkness into the bookcases above me. A sound-shadow passed over my ear, stirring the hairs on the back of my neck.

I sat up and shuddered. Down the hall, faintly, a woman was speaking and another singing. Was it Babette again? I hoped so. I got out of bed and made my way to the library door. This time the sound, a kind of twangling, was coming from the opposite end of the corridor, to my left. I glided along the corridor like a floating thing in the direction of the sound.

The lights of the creamy salon were on. I stopped to peer in, and the room seemed narrower. In place of the grand piano stood a slender white harpsichord. My great-aunt's portrait had narrowed too, making her look longer. In fact, it was a room of slender things *for* slender things, for the spines of things rather than the things themselves, for sylphs and swans and splintered things, things to move among, not settle on.

I did not enter the room but moved on, resuming my glide. At the end of the hall, a door was ajar. It was the solarium, but it was mooned over at this hour—making it a lunarium instead, I guess. My great-aunt was inside, dressed in a primrose nightgown, her hair still up but her face shiny with cream. A single lamp, a tulip looking down, cast the room in an amber light. My great-aunt stood and swayed to the pretty music, a soft aria. Her eyes closed, her expression swoony, her shiny face glowing, arms hugged across her and warped hands open and gloveless, each cupping a shoulder. She had become a glowhead. She spoke to the record as she swayed. She said, "Lie down in your own green meadow, your *verdi prati,* my Handel, my everlasting George." I took an extra look around the room. She made me nervous. She spoke about the composer's wig, asking him to lie down with her, calling him "my George F. H." She asked him to lie down in the grass and sing one of his own sad songs. She said, "Has someone disappointed you, lambkin? Is that it? Who is your unfaithful woman? The woman who pulled a shadow over your meadow?" Hermina turned toward me but did not see me. Her eyes were silken. She said, "What young woman sat for you or what cut boy"— Hermina put her curved hand to her own throat—"sang your *Messiah,* intoning your 'He Shall Feed His Flock'? And to what far meadow did that flock wander?"

At the end of the song, Hermina turned toward the door and finally noticed me. I expected her to yelp or jump with embarrassment, but she didn't do either, not at all. She beckoned instead. "Come in, my dear."

I hesitated at first—I was once again the one who felt embarrassed—but Hermina came to get me, hugged me with her bare hands. "Handel gave regret a sound," she said into my head and smoothed my hair at the back. People spoke a lot into the top of my head. "Do you know what I'm saying?" she asked, holding my face now. "Can you hear it?"

"I am very young," I said in response.

"Ha!" she said, releasing me. "You were never young. You were born old." She approached the phonograph and found a record already out of its sleeve. "Let's listen to a song together," she said and put it on top of the one that had been playing. "My Ede would be appalled. His records were pristine, but I'm much too hungry to keep them that way." She chuckled. I hoped she might replace some of the records my grandmother had lost.

I sat and listened. It was cool in the lunarium, but the amber lamp warmed the room like a hearth. I sank into a soft, ample chair.

"This record is Handel's *Teseo,*" my great-aunt said. "Dame Martha Bolingbroke plays the part of Medea." Hermina was already swaying again, though she had not yet found the song she wanted. But she stopped herself, came over, and took my face in her bird hands again. The whites of her eyes were big and silver. I didn't know what to expect. "Do you know who Medea was?" she asked.

I shook my head, freeing my face from her clutches.

"Medea was married to Jason, the leader of the ancient Argonauts. She had two children with him, but he betrayed her." Hermina was shaking her head but saying yes. "Oh, yes, he betrayed her. He left Medea for another woman, and when he left, Medea murdered her own children so that he could not enjoy them either. It was the ultimate revenge."

I sat up in my chair, wondering if I should leave, feeling I might. My great-aunt turned her shining face away from me and found the song. "This is the only recording of this sublime opera, made in 1915 in London, right in the middle of the Great War, some two centuries after Mr. Handel himself premiered it in the same city. Listen," she said, her face glowing. "Medea is addressing her children after she has slashed their throats."

I put my hand up to my own throat and sat up straight. "What are their names?"

"They are called Mermeros and Pheres."

I repeated the names. They sounded musical.

My great-aunt said, "She wants them to have a sweet sleep—a *dolce riposo*. Listen to Dame Martha. Her voice is as dark as a well."

Dolce riposo, ed innocente pace . . .

The dark voice sang the words as Hermina's humming rode aboard it. The song was beautiful, sad but beautiful. I was riveted. I felt carried back to a time before letters and reading when, like the ancients, I could remember every word that was sung or spoken, in whatever language—the sound of the words, if not their meaning— just by hearing the song.

"Oh, yes, Medea," my great-aunt said to the record. "Yes, yes, the one and only Medea." She was swaying and swooning again. "Oh, yes, revenge." My great-aunt turned to me. "Sweet revenge. How can I ever repay you for your acts of cruelty?" Hermina held up her curved hands to the moonlight. "Look at me," she said. "Look what you have done." She was gazing up in the lunarium. "How glorious it would be to exact such revenge." I didn't know who she meant, who she was talking to. "Single-minded Medea," she said to the record. "Can there ever be a cost more dear than the lives of your children? Did you taste their blood, the iron in it, all the lamb they'd been eating, the sweetness of the red grapes?" Hermina was alone now with the song, alone in the room. "It is the best drink in the world," she said.

"Better than Hitler could drink, better than Stalin and Mussolini and Genghis Khan and Vlad the Impaler put together. Did any one of them dare gas himself, starve himself, freeze himself, cut off his own head, impale himself? Not one. But you dared, Medea. You drank your own blood's blood. You humbled them all. You dared."

And then someone coughed, someone in the middle of the crackling recording made in the middle of the First World War, someone in that London concert hall, someone listening to Dame Martha sing tenderly about sweet sleep to her murdered children, coughed. Then he coughed again, a cough as loud as the song. Did the man have a cold, back there in 1915? Was he a smoker? Where did he take his smoke? Maybe he took it in a café like Gerbeaud, over a hand of cards, or in a tavern over a beer and a conversation about the world coming apart, or maybe it was in a room like this, a salon after dinner, while he was drinking brandy with men who wanted to talk about the Terrible War. Maybe he passed out Sobranie Black Russian cigarettes with the gold foil filter, the kind Hermina smoked, and sometimes Mamu too. Maybe he kept them behind a garter in a monogrammed silver cigarette case, just like my grandmother's. And then one night the gentleman traveled with his darling by carriage to the opera in London to listen to Dame Martha sing this song of horror, the song of Medea, and heard for the first time in this dark voice that even a murderer could be tender.

The song was just finishing. "What happened to you, Aunt Hermina?"

157

She turned. She looked at me calmly. I was a little scared.

"What happened?" she repeated.

"Please tell me what happened to you, to your fingers." Her bare fingers looked curved and red, but nothing more, nothing horrible. "Why do you wear all those gloves?"

She smiled at me, took my face into her hands again. "You know," she said, "it's not a story for the ages."

"I don't know what you mean," I said. "I'm not asking for a story for the ages. I'm asking what happened to you."

She let my face go and looked down at her hands, held them up to the amber light of the tulip lamp for both of us to look at, as if they belonged to someone else. I glanced at my own hands and wanted suddenly to hide them, to sit on them.

"Before you and your brother were born, back in 1941, we had it just so, back in Budapest, my Ede and I. There were the anti-Jewish laws, of course, and we had lost some things—Hungary was allied with Germany, as you probably know." I nodded. "But Ede had been able to keep his posting as a doctor, and so there were deprivations, but we had it better than most. We had our circle of friends; we had my brothers and sisters— your grandmother—and their families; we had our walks in the park and our coffees, our celebrations, if a little quieter than before, our weddings, births, our holidays, the usual." She looked down into her lap, at her hands. "That's partly because your uncle Ede was invaluable as a surgeon. He wrote the book on it—*books*. They are used to this day in German and French and English teaching hospitals. So we, especially, had it just so. And then one day in the winter of 1941—December sixteenth, to be exact—they came to get us."

"They came to *get* you? Who did?"

My great-aunt put my hands in the warm claws of hers. "Germans, German soldiers. They burst into our home near the river—you know, near the Elizabeth Bridge." Hermina swallowed. "They came in the middle of the night, turned on the lights, tore us out of bed. They would not let us get our things, would not let us dress. I was still in my nightgown. They took us down, out into the freezing wind, to a black car, a Mercedes, waiting in front of our building. Then they injected us with something. I barely had time to see where my Ede was sitting before I lost consciousness. When we woke— it had to have been seven or eight or nine hours later— we were pulling up in Munich, in Germany, at a military hospital. It was colder there than in Hungary, as cold a day as I can remember, but they hustled us inside. They put a surgeon's gown over Ede's pajamas and told him he had to operate on a wounded officer, who turned out to be Josef Dortmund, Colonel Josef Dortmund, of the Alsace region. I stood there in the cold corridor in my nightgown, trembling and humiliated. I thought that we were finished, that we had no hope. I told Ede, in Hungarian, of course, not to operate on him, not to make these German officers well so they could go back to their killing, starting with us. And I said it without even knowing the full extent of their killing yet. We had no idea. Only an inkling."

My great-aunt was looking down again at her lap, her hands. She was trying not to show me that she had begun to cry. I wasn't sure what to do.

"They took us to a window overlooking a courtyard with an iron cable strung across it. The sky above it was gray. One of the German officers said to me, in fluent Hungarian, that he had heard what I'd said. He looked Ede in the eye and told him that they were going to hang me out there in the yard by my fingertips while Ede performed the surgery and would not let me down until he was finished. He begged them not to. He promised he would do the surgery. The same officer said, 'Yes, you will do it, and you will do it while your wife waits for you out there.' And so they made Ede watch as they pushed me out onto a platform, fastened my fingertips to the cable with steel clamps, pushed me out to dangle above the winter courtyard, and even ran water along the cable to freeze my fingers. It was so methodical, as if they were just hanging out laundry. At first I was in shrieking pain. I kept looking up at them, imploring them. I trembled violently. I begged my fingers to release me, let me fall, let me shatter on the cobblestones below me.

"And then something happened. I don't know if it was minutes or an hour or two hours later. I'd been shaking, everything about me clattering, my bones, my stone body, when all of a sudden I felt myself calm down. The noise and violence, the ringing in my ears, it all stopped, and I actually felt at peace—warm, if that were possible."

Hermina looked at me, the lamp lighting up her face, scaring me slightly. I couldn't get a sound out of my throat.

"I went to a place beyond things," Hermina said. "Beyond the sound. It was quiet and painless. Even the sky seemed to soften. I believe I smiled. Can you imagine how I must have horrified my tormentors!"

Hermina stopped talking. Her breath evened out. She took my hands in hers again. I gazed down at her fingers, searching for the evidence, imagining the scene of the crime.

"Please go on," I said.

"That was not a story for a young man," she said. "I'm sorry." She looked me straight in the eyes, a tender look, one I recognized. My grandmother had that look.

"But I've never been young. That's what you told me."

"When I woke," she went on, "I was in a hospital bed, quite a nice one. My Ede was beside me, kissing me over and over, speaking softly to me. I could hear his voice even before I could wake. I thought I might have been elsewhere. When I was fully awake, he looked so happy, relieved. My hands were in bandages, and for whatever reason my forehead and cheeks were too. It was days later—several days. A few minutes later, in came the German colonel in a wheelchair, pushed by a nurse. 'How is the patient?' he asked, as if I'd had a fall, an accident. I was back, Ede said. I was alive. The colonel told me he was a great admirer of mine. 'You have a strange way of showing it,' I told him. The colonel was going to say something else, but he couldn't. He clasped his hands together. He looked down and then away before retreating.

"By Christmas Day I was a bit better. I was sitting up, taking meals, with help, of course. I was asked by a nurse, who spoke a little Hungarian, if I was well enough to move a little, to leave my room, perhaps. I answered in German that I was. She wheeled me down to a small chapel attached to the hospital. The colonel was there in full regalia with his wife and his beautiful boy, maybe half your age, and several other officers. A piano accompanist, a young woman not much bigger than a sparrow, awaited me. And of course Ede was there, and he stood to assist me. He whispered to me that the colonel had asked for a song." Hermina was shaking her head. "Imagine. Maybe I was dead after all and in heaven. But what was the colonel doing there with me? I was to sing now. One day, I was to be hung out by my fingertips to freeze or to die, and now I was to sing. I looked around at the chapel, and, strangely, there were no Christian symbols to be seen. Jesus on his cross behind me was covered over with a bedsheet. Even the altar was draped over."

"Did they do that for you?" I asked.

"No, of course not. They would never have done that for me. They covered up Christ for Hitler. His kingdom was a one-man show.

"So the young pianist came up to me and gently asked what I might like to sing. I studied the faces of my little audience and told her that 'for Christmas' I wanted to sing an English carol. Did she know 'Once in Royal

David's City'? She said she did. And so, with my Ede by my side, my voice smaller than usual but as strong as I could make it, I sang. Do you know the song?" she asked me. "We sing it in Hungarian. I'll do it for you."

Hermina closed her eyes, placed her hands on her heart, and sang the song for me with the same small voice.

Once in royal David's city
Stood a lowly cattle shed,
Where a mother laid her baby
In a manger for his bed;
Mary was that mother mild,
Jesus Christ her little child.

And our eyes at last shall see him,
Through his own redeeming love;
For that child so dear and gentle
Is our Lord in heaven above;
And he leads his children on,
To the place where he is gone.

Not in that poor, lowly stable,
With the oxen standing by,
Shall we see him, but in heaven,
Set at God's right hand on high;
Then like stars his children, crowned,
All in white, his praise will sound!

"And then do you know what I did, my darling boy?" She opened her eyes so wide it was like extra sound was coming from them. She was beaming. "I was looking straight at the young blond boy, who seemed very pleased with my song. My Ede bent down, I whispered a request to him, and then he marched over to the Jesus on the cross and pulled the drapery off him with a flourish, like a magician."

FOURTEEN

I WOKE WITH THE weight of the world on my chest. I couldn't breathe. We have a heavy planet. I opened my eyes. Attila was sitting on my chest.

"Wake up, *mon petit chou*."

"Get off me." I tried to push him off.

His head was right up against the bookcase. He was already fully dressed. "Wake up, my little plum dumpling. I want to show you something." He gave me a Pez for breakfast, one from his Scarecrow, very generous.

"Are we going to see Paris?" I asked.

"Not yet, my pumpkin loaf," he said. "Just come with me." I put on yesterday's clothes while Attila told me I had an important mission ahead of me. Then he said, "You were born twelve thousand years after the last ice age, twelve thousand years since the end of the Pleistocene epoch."

"Exactly?" I asked. "So were you born eleven thousand, nine hundred and ninety-six years after the last ice age?"

"Come, my little imbecile, my birdling."

My brother led me downstairs. We stole toward the back of the house, past the bright solarium and outside. It was still damp after the night's heavy rain, but the sun was shining.

Attila took me to a small white house, which had gables ornamented with gingerbread trim. It looked like a fairy-tale house, but it turned out to be a shed. He pushed open the door. The lock had been jimmied. I examined it for a moment and looked at my brother.

"When did you find this place?" I asked.

"While you were sleeping," he said. "Wait until you see what's in here."

"What is it?"

"I just said wait, my frolicsome puppy."

The shed was full of household objects: a tarnished silver tray, several vases, lamp shades, shelves of things, overloaded like the bookcases in the library, a chaise longue, as well as old lamps, a small writing desk, like a student's slope-top desk, with its lid unhinged on one side, and, sprawled out on the floor, a grand crystal chandelier, waiting to rise again.

A doctor's bag stood by the door. We opened it to find it loaded with good things: a stethoscope, a thermometer, syringes, reflex hammers, a blood-pressure cuff, a nifty flashlight, which Attila beamed straight into my eye, a brilliant assortment of scissors, one of which he clacked menacingly near my ear, and a small silver saw.

"These are great," I said. "I wonder what Uncle Ede used this for?" I was holding up the gleaming saw.

"To cut through bone, probably."

I gazed in horror at the instrument in my hand, tried to spot traces of blood on it.

"This is not why we're here, though," my brother said. "Not for this stuff. I'll do a full examination of the rest of it later, with your cooperation, naturally. Though this could come in handy," he said and pocketed the flashlight.

Attila led me to the room's main treasure: a great black leather chest sitting in the far corner. It too had a lock, and it too had been jimmied. The surface of the chest was carved with images of men wearing safari hats, riding camels. Lions, zebras, and gazelles watched as the parade of humans went by, one man wearing spectacles, one smoking a pipe, one with his arm raised, holding forth about the world, it looked like. I ran my hand over the figures cut into the soft black leather. My brother lifted the lid. Inside were packets of things, including several thick sheaves of papers and photographs bundled with ribbon.

"Are we supposed to be going through this stuff?" I asked.

"I don't know—*you* decide."

He handed me some official-looking papers, like passports, but they were yellow and blue. They were written in a strange language, and each had the word *Schutz-Pass* on it, and, below that, the word *Schweden* topped with three crowns.

"What are these?" I asked as I looked at a photograph of an unfamiliar face on one of them. It was a man, looking slightly bewildered. The next one had a photo of a woman, again unfamiliar. I didn't know what to make of the documents, though it did feel exciting just to be holding them, especially here in the secrecy of the shed.

"Are you ready for these?" Attila said. He handed me four other documents, blue and yellow like the others.

At first I didn't know what he expected me to notice. I felt I was being tested. But then my eyes fell upon the unmistakable face of our father. I flipped to the next *Schutz-Pass*. It was our mother's. Her name was there in plain sight: Lili Beck. And then Attila's! "*Son:* Attila Beck," it said, along with his birth date.

"There's no picture of you," I said.

Attila shook his head. "I was just *son of* then. It was before I became a Titan."

I turned back to my father's picture, stamped with a royal seal, glanced again at the three crowns and the word *Schweden* below. There were two other such documents with photos of our grandparents. Mamu was a little younger and even thinner, more like Hermina now, and my grandfather was older than in the photos I'd seen. His hair, here, was white.

"Now look at the signatures below," Attila said. "Can you read them?"

Above the signatures were three words printed in another language, then translated into Hungarian:

Königlich Schwedische Gesandtschaft
Svéd Királyi Követség

"It's signed on behalf of the Swedish king," Attila said solemnly.

I tried to make out one of the signatures on my grandfather's pass. "R. Wallen—"

"Raoul Wallenberg!" Attila said, slapping at the *Schutz-Passes* in my hand. "Now look at these," he said and pointed to the passes of our parents.

"How did Aunt Hermina get hold of our parents' and grandparents' passes?"

"You'll find out soon, my curious little kitten."

The signature on them was even more difficult to decipher. I could make out a *P* in the first name and a *B* in the second, but what a hurried scrawl it was.

"Paul Beck!" Attila shouted, angry, punching my shoulder from behind. "Look at it." And when I did, I saw that he was right. I wondered why Paul Beck hadn't been taught to write with better penmanship. He would not have gotten away with it in Mrs. Molnar's class.

"The mystery man," I said.

"Do you know what these are?" Attila said. "They're official documents. It makes our parents and grandparents and me *Swedish!*"

"We're not Swedish," I said lamely.

"Of course not, my little monkey boot." My brother jammed the passes at me and rummaged through the other bundles of papers and photographs. He got right down on his knees with his head inside the trunk.

So these were our confidence men, Raoul Wallenberg and Paul Beck, our family's own secret men.

"Look," Attila said. He handed me a photo of Hermina with our grandmother and maybe Agi, their sister, and four other women, all of them in their teens. "Look at *this*," he said, a moment later. It was a grainy photo of a boy bound to a man back-to-back with heavy rope. They were standing on a bridge with some guards holding them by the neck. I couldn't tell which bridge it was, but the parliament buildings in the background meant that it was the Danube and Budapest.

"What was going on?" I asked.

"I don't know," my brother said.

Another photo showed a long lineup of well-dressed people. The street looked familiar, Terez Boulevard, possibly. And there was another picture of a man seated at a card table, the table set among people on the sidewalk. The man was signing a document.

"Now look at *this*," my brother said. He had moved on to the next exhibit. It was a belt with a bold silver buckle featuring a powerful eagle standing on a bicycle wheel with the spokes bent. A swastika. Three words I could not understand were inscribed above the bird: *Gott mit Uns*.

"What does it mean?" I asked.

"I don't know; it's German," Attila said. He was still foraging. He handed me a postcard. On the front was a colorful picture of an army truck with a swastika painted on its side. It was not being driven but pulled by a horse with bleeding hooves. A soldier walked alongside the vehicle. He wore a torn and patched uniform with the Iron Cross dangling from his neck but flung to the back instead of the front. At the bottom of the photo was the caption L'ALLEMAGNE, 1945. I turned the postcard over. Someone had written on the back:

Edward et Hermina,
  Vive les Alliés! Merci pour la délivrance!
           —Mancus

Attila handed me a yellow piece of paper. "Look at all the languages the Crow Woman speaks."

"Don't call her that," I said.

My brother glared at me.

"It's not necessary," I added.

I looked at the paper. I tried to sound out the word printed in bold at the head of the document: *Arbeitsnach-weis.* Typed into the space left blank on the paper were names I recognized: "Dr. Edward and Hermina Izsak." I stared intently at the last word before pronouncing it: "Izsak."

"Edward is Uncle Ede," my brother said, his voice muffled by the trunk. "And Izsak is the surname, Ede and Hermina's."

Before I knew it, I was holding a yellow cloth badge with a star on it, a six-pointed one, like the one on our temple back home and at the head of the gate of my grandfather's cemetery. As I ran the cloth badge between my fingers, my brother said, "You can pin it on later as a crappy sheriff's badge, and I'll wear the buckle.

I'll be the outlaw, and you can try to arrest me, if you can catch me."

Attila thrust another document at me. It was entitled *Evacuation de Paris—Instructions pour la population.*

An airplane roared over our heads. Then I heard rustling outside. "We have to go now," I said.

"Not just yet." My brother withdrew a packet of letters tied with a blue ribbon. "Look at these," he said. The handwriting was familiar to me, the soft loops, the swooping lines, like embroidery. They were from our grandmother. I could even tell which pen she'd used, my grandfather Robert's famous 1924 Waterman fountain pen, which he'd kept in the middle drawer of his mahogany desk and which we'd all gotten to try. The pen had outlasted my grandfather. I hoped somebody had brought it with us from Budapest. The letters were from our grandmother to Hermina.

"Sit down," my brother told me. I pulled up a little footstool and sat. He took out the top letter and eyed it feverishly. "Listen," he said. "*Listen.*"

1 Jokai Street
Budapest, Hungary
18 July 1945

My dear Hermi,
Our Paul did something that looms over these days like some kind of monument, the way tall Paul does over each of us. I am sorry that I have not been able to share the story with anyone, even you, Hermi, until now. We're

always worried about who might read the letter and what the consequences might be.

I don't know how much information made it out to you, so you might or might not know that Paul was helping the Swedish diplomat Raoul Wallenberg issue false papers to Jews here in Budapest. They were agents of heaven, the two of them, and they were fearless. Jews and Gypsies were being rounded up and marched to train stations for deportation, sometimes to Auschwitz, where so many of us perished, Hermi. Our poor Lajos, as you know. Poor Agi. And Magda, and her boy Bandi—do you remember how he played piano—composed for the piano at 13 and 14? I can't think of it.

So Mr. Wallenberg would set up a small folding table at the station and from a briefcase he'd brought with him pull out files and set them out neatly, like a notary, 60 or 70 or 75 newly minted Swedish passports each time, in alphabetical order, complete with photographs. Our Paul was his sidekick, a deputized Swedish diplomat himself, with his own false papers, like ours.

There was disorder at the station, as you can imagine. I say "disorder" rather than "chaos" because our captors managed it all with the butts of their rifles. Sometimes, though, there was a din on the platform, and Mr. Wallenberg would have trouble delaying the proceedings, so Paul would climb to the top of the train itself and blow a whistle. Imagine it. He'd blow his shrill whistle and, when he got people's attention, captors and captives alike, he'd announce that there were 70 (or however many) Swedish nationals on board and that the Swedish officials

(Paul and Mr. Wallenberg) demanded their release. The Germans would cooperate, since they were the ones who had proclaimed that they were deporting certain groups and certain groups only, but certainly not Swedes.

One day Simon, Lili, our little Attila, my Robert, and I were rounded up and marched away. That day, strangely, we saw no sign of Paul or Mr. Wallenberg. We were crammed into a windowless car with hundreds of others. It was this time last year, a hot July day. I felt especially sorry for my dear husband, who had never known anything but the most respectful treatment—and don't you know all about that, you and your dear Ede? Yet he didn't say a word. We were all in shock, I guess. Surprisingly, even our usually restless little grandson was subdued that day. I can't imagine what he was thinking. Better not to know.

To head us off, our Paul borrowed a Swedish embassy car, an Alfa Romeo, no less, from Mr. Wallenberg. He had heard from his sister that we had been taken. He drove a good distance out of Budapest, parked the car across the train tracks, got out, and waited for our train to approach and come to a stop.

Hermi, try to picture it: the train stopped, the Einsatzkommando got off, along with a few officers, and Paul told the commander that they had four Swedish nationals, plus a boy, on board and that he demanded their release. He presented our papers to the commander. The officer looked Paul over, heard his perfect German, without even a trace of a Hungarian accent, or, for that matter, Swedish one, and walked down the row of cars, sliding open one door after another. The German called out, "Beck! Robert, Klari, Simon, Lili, Attila!" No one on board knew if it was a good thing or bad to be a Beck at that moment. It was generally not a good thing to be singled out. Usually it was not to receive a reward that your name was being called.

Imagine our surprise when our door was thrown open and the sun fell on us. As our eyes adjusted, we could see Paul standing there, wearing his camel-hair cape and panama hat. His clothes were too warm for the weather, but with his cornflower eyes and the tipsy red curls beneath the brim of his hat, he looked every bit the Swede he was playing.

We wanted to shout "Hallelujah!" but of course couldn't and didn't. We couldn't give any sign that we knew the man in the cape, and Lili right away signaled Attila to be quiet. The child looked scared. The four of us knew right away what role we were to play, and Attila might have sensed it too, I suppose.

The officer told me to get down. I understood aussteigen. *The five of us worked our way to the door. Simon helped me down to the gravel. Then he helped Attila and Lili and his father. The officer studied our faces and compared them to the photographs on the papers Paul had given him. Lili's picture had been placed strategically on top, since she is blond and blue-eyed. And then there was her blond boy with her. Finally, the commander told us we could go.*

Well, you won't believe it, Hermi. Paul asked the man if they had taken our valuables. The commander

*said yes. So Paul asked for them back. We couldn't be-
lieve what we were hearing. The officer looked at Paul
and then his eyes ranged over our faces. The man told his
junior officer to go get our things. The man ran to fetch a
burlap sack. Paul said to us in German, and in a voice as
cool as the commander's, that we should find our jewelry.*

*Robert looked in the sack, reached in, and pulled out a
pocket watch. He read the inscription on the back and
slipped the watch into his vest pocket. I combed through
the bag and took out an emerald pin, which I held up to
the light before fastening the brooch to my chest. It went
with my rose jacket perfectly, though it was not mine. Simon shook his head when the sack was passed to him,
and then the sack went to Lili. Simon took Attila from
her arms.*

*They had taken her wedding ring, so she reached into
the bag and tried on several rings before finding one that
fit. When she did, she slipped it on and smiled.*

*Lili still has that ring, and she wears it as her wedding
ring, though it is inscribed "Ivan. 13 Aprilis 1935." I
wonder if Ivan—the poor man—and his wife ever made
it back.*

*Paul helped each of us into the Alfa Romeo, and he did
so in the most patient and civil manner imaginable, considering we were holding up the train run by the Germans.
The car was cream-colored. It matched Paul's outfit. He
drove us back to Budapest to a building annexed by the
Swedes, and we lived out the remaining months of the war
in an office. I have enclosed the Schutz-Passes so you can
see what kind of operation it was.*

*My dear Hermi, even as I recall those days and relive
them, it's hard for me to believe that we were once so
trapped and so near the end of things. Of life! I know
your own personal chapter was even bigger, considerably
darker. Yet here we are, all of us. We made it, Hermi,
and you are still singing. And your Ede was allowed to
continue his good work.*

*Paul doesn't say much about you, I'm afraid, but he
doesn't say much about anything. While most people are
trying to get on with their lives, he spends his time here
with us, in Robert's study with the lights switched off and
the curtains drawn, most often, and he hardly stirs, even
when we call him for a meal. He must be wondering
about his hero and ours, Mr. Wallenberg, who was taken
somewhere by the Russians in January, from Debrecen,
and has not been seen since. But more than Paul's hero,
Mr. Wallenberg was his mentor, his inspiration. There
was no going back to the simple practice of law after what
Paul had accomplished under Mr. Wallenberg's tutelage. I
sometimes think that for someone who bore so much, it's
sad that Paul is not able now to bear the weight of his
thoughts. Still, I will tell him I have reported to you
about him and his circumstances.*

*His sister Rozsi is here with us too. Poor thing is wait-
ing for Tibor, her fiancé, to return from the war. He was
taken as well, but the Swedes and their helpers could not
save him. With each passing day, we become less hopeful.*

*Paul did give me permission to write to you both, the
aunt and uncle he most admires, I believe. I would say he
might even have been pleased that I was willing to do so.*

Hermi, when I think of you, it makes me happy to know that people are singing again.

I send fondest good wishes and love from all of us to you and to dear Ede.

with my love,
Klari

Attila looked up at me. He'd read the letter like a trained actor, gripped by it. His eyes were red and bursting.

"Do you remember?" I asked.

"Not a thing," Attila said, his voice cracked now. "I was practically a baby. I wonder what happened to Aunt Hermina and Uncle Ede. Why was their chapter worse?"

I shrugged my shoulders. I couldn't tell Attila. I didn't know what he would do.

Attila folded the letter methodically and tucked it back into its envelope. He added the *Schutz-Passes,* then slipped the envelope into his back pocket. He tied the blue ribbon around the rest of the little bundle, placed it all back in the trunk, closed the lid, and then, without saying a word, shot out of the shed like a bird. I had to run after him, rushing to close the door of the shed behind me, slipping, almost, on a patch of mud.

Inside, he was searching for our father. Our mother, grandmother, and Babette were in the large kitchen with its sunny windows.

When my brother joined us, our mother asked where we'd been. "Don't disappear like that," she said, "please, my darlings." She took each of us in her arms, but Attila broke away.

Babette was standing by to make my brother and me an omelet. She and our mother were beaming out smiles like rapiers back and forth across the kitchen.

Attila was shifting his weight from one foot to the other. If cartoon speech balloons had been shooting out of his head, they'd have contained only exclamation points and question marks. "Where's Dad?" he asked. "Where is he?"

"He's out," our grandmother said. "What is the matter with you? Why don't you sit down?"

"I'd rather stand on my own legs," he said. He actually snorted and stamped his foot. "What about Aunt Hermina?" he burst out. "Why did she have it worse than we did? How could you have it worse than being placed on a death train and then hiding out in an office building?"

My mother got to her feet. Her smile was gone. "How do you know that?"

Attila stamped his foot again. "What really did happen to Paul Beck?" he asked. "We were in Hungary for eleven years after Paul left. We were under Russian rule. The Russians came to our house. They kicked us out. They let us slip out of the country, though they didn't care for our men, Raoul Wallenberg and Paul. What is it about this story that doesn't add up? Help me, O Lord, to see the logic of your ways. Help me, O humans."

"Your father will be back any minute," our mother said. "He's been out with Aunt Hermina, making some arrangements for our departure. He's under a great deal of strain. Please don't add to it by asking your questions. There will be time enough for everything."

"What did Aunt Hermina mean about Dad's cousin?" Attila said, snorting again as he did. He clenched a fist. "What could he have stopped? Where did Paul go? Where is he? Has anybody ever seen him again?"

"Why are you cross-examining us?" our mother said.

"Because I want to know."

"Don't you think we want to know more too?"

Babette approached my brother, not knowing what was being said but understanding the tone. She took my brother's chin in her hand and smiled at him until he took a deep breath. Then she set to work making our eggs, aiming her breasts at the stove, where they could serve little purpose.

"We want to know as much as you do, dear," Mamu said. "We've been looking for Paul for years. We don't know what became of him, but we're hoping. We've looked everywhere. He was strong-headed enough to go hunting for Raoul Wallenberg in Siberia, for all we know."

"But he was with us in our house. Wasn't Paul with us in our house? What happened? Where did he go? *Why* did he go?"

"Yes, Paul was in our house," our grandmother said, "and his sister Rozsi too. Their own town house in Budapest had been destroyed. But please, let's take this into the other room."

We left Babette and moved down the hall to the solarium. My mother, grandmother, and I sat on a low flowered divan while my brother paced back and forth in front of us.

"I need to know everything that happened," Attila said. "What happened to Paul and to Rozsi?"

"Why do you have to know this now?" asked our mother. "I'm trying my best to keep you and your brother from harm, but you won't let me. You fight me and your father."

My brother stopped, took our mother by the shoulders, and said, "You're not protecting us from harm by keeping this from us."

Our mother glanced at our grandmother, who looked down. Our mother got to her feet. "I'll tell you if you sit down."

"I want to stand."

She looked Attila dead in the eye. "I will tell you if you sit down."

He plopped himself down beside me, where she'd been sitting, and she stayed on her feet.

"You're not going to like this story," she said.

"Then why do you insist on telling it?" Mamu said. "They have plenty of time to find out."

"They've earned it, Mother. They've come such a long way on this journey with us."

Our grandmother sighed and leaned back, but the soft divan had no back to rest against and she sat forward again.

"It was after the war," our mother began.

"Right after?" Attila asked.

"Not right after, but soon after, in forty-six. Robert, Dr. Beck, your grandfather, came home from his clinic one day to find Paul in his—your grandfather's—study.

Paul spent a great deal of time in there. His sister Rozsi was prancing around the living room, saying she'd finally found herself a pair of nylon stockings. She had drawn seams up the back of her legs with an eyebrow pencil, and I must say, the lines were drawn with some skill, because they looked quite straight, and in dim light you might have thought she was wearing stockings. I had arranged at the druggist for Rozsi to have sedatives, because every time we went looking for her fiancé, Tibor, at the train station and didn't find him, she despaired. Her Tibor had been taken away and never came back."

"Who took him away?" I asked.

"The Germans took him. He was deported. The deal back then, *after* the war—I mean the law, actually— was that two able-bodied people from each family, if the family had two able-bodied people left in it, would have to go out to rebuild the city. We each had our assignments. I was helping clean up the National Gallery, which was damaged, and your father was helping to rebuild the Chain Bridge across the Danube. The Germans had bombed all the bridges. You were already with us, my darling," she said to my brother. "But we hadn't started on you yet," she said to me and smiled. I blushed. "So your father and I went on this work detail each day, and Paul and Rozsi did not." Mamu was shaking her head, wishing our mother would stop.

"Who looked after me?" Attila asked.

"Your grandmother."

A cloud passed from above the solarium, and the room

lit up. My brother shut his right eye. "Why didn't Paul and Rozsi go?" he asked.

"I don't know. To this day, I don't know for sure. Rozsi was depressed. Her man was gone and would not return. Paul was depressed. His hero—*and ours*—was gone. I don't know. But I didn't care. Paul had saved us."

The room clouded over again. It felt cooler, all of a sudden. The white radiator was ticking.

"Your father and I were happy to go. You were growing like a weed, but we had your grandmother to look after you, as I said. It didn't seem a problem for us. We'd made it—whoever was left of us. My parents did not survive. My brothers and sisters did not survive. But we did. You did and we did. We were alive. We could make it work.

"But the arrangement was not sitting right with your grandfather. And one night at dinner, after some months together, he asked Paul if he and Rozsi were ever going out on the work detail in place of us. 'They have a child now,' he said to them. 'They want to have another one.'" Paul told him that he didn't think so. "We went on eating quietly for what felt like several minutes, several awful minutes, until your grandfather put down his fork, wiped his mouth, and told Paul he thought he and his sister should go out on work detail the following day. "Paul wiped his mouth too and finished chewing. He replied, 'And what if we refuse?'

"Your grandfather said, 'Then I think you and your sister should leave.'"

The radiator seemed all of a sudden to be working extra hard. I felt flushed, raised a cool hand to my cheek. Mamu put her arm around me.

"Then what?" Attila said and started to get to his feet. The room brightened again. His eyes were blazing blue.

Our mother put a hard hand on his shoulder. "Stay there," she said. "I'm telling you the story."

For once my brother obeyed.

"In the middle of that night..." She paused. My grandmother removed her arm from around me and covered her face with her hands. "In the middle of the night, Paul and his sister left."

I could feel my grandmother's body trembling. She was still covering her face.

"That night was the last time we saw them or heard from them," our mother said. She held her hands together under her chin, as if she were praying. Her eyes were welling up too. "There was no trace of them, not anywhere near their own house, which had taken a direct hit, not in Paul's old law office, not in his usual haunts, like the New York Café and Gerbeaud. We caught up with his brother Istvan in Szeged, and he told your grandparents that Paul did not want to be found. He and Rozsi were gone. They had left for the Americas, as Istvan put it. We thought, actually, that Paul might have come here to Paris. He adored his aunt. We thought they might stop here on their way to something."

"To *what*?" Attila shouted. Now my brother did stand up. He turned to our grandmother. "Mamu," he snapped. She pulled her hands from her face. "Your hus-

184

band banished the man who saved our lives, and a decade later we're sitting around guessing where he might have gotten to?"

"I'm sure he was looking for something," our mother cut in. "He would have been trouble to the Russians, the way Wallenberg was. Wallenberg was a subversive where the authorities were concerned—whatever authorities. That's all the Russians cared about. Make order. Clear out the rabble-rousers. Clear out subversives, trouble-makers. Paul would be on the warpath. There was no proof Wallenberg died. There still isn't. We don't know what happened. Paul would still be agitating. He would still be a menace, if he could be."

"And that's *it?*" Attila slapped at the air.

I ducked, thinking he might connect with one of us.

"You have some of Paul's qualities," our mother said to Attila.

"Is that so?" he said. He was fuming.

"What about me?" I asked.

"Actually—" my mother began to say, when Attila interrupted.

"*Actually,* you were named after our grandfather, the man who evicted Paul from our house, the man who banished our savior."

"Attila! Why would you say that to your brother? You don't know who to be angry at."

"He is Robert, is he not? I'm angry at all of you—all of *us!*"

I took off to our bedroom in the library and slammed the door. I threw myself down on the daybed underneath the shelves of books, hoping they'd collapse and bury me in their considerations.

Of course I knew I'd been named after our grandfather, but now it seemed I had not been named Robert so much as *branded*. In how many ways could a single soul be branded? It was hard enough being an earthling, receiving the light of dead stars, but to be a branded earthling, a marked earthling. To be 9.8 and relegated to childhood and childish ways and questions was one thing, but to be a Hungarian, or maybe not even a Hungarian, a Jew, a boy on the run, to have seen my redheaded cousin die at the foot of a lamppost, and a man with combed hair—also red—hanged, and another with his hat blown away, complete with his head, to have pictured a dear great-aunt hung out on a frozen line, to have longed hopelessly for a pretty nun with a soft white neck in a convent in Austria, or even a girl with banana-string hair and delicious lips who would end up in another section of heaven, a better section, no doubt; to have watched our father beat a propeller judge, these were brands enough. But to have been made a Robert too, not a Paul, not a Raoul, not even an Attila, but a Robert, the man who'd banished our savior—this was a branding meant to burn deep.

I had my back to the door, my arm folded over my face, when my mother and grandmother slipped into the room. My mother kissed me on my temple and smiled her starry smile at me. My grandmother gently waved my mother away, and my mother kissed me again in the same spot before departing. "It will all be good, I promise," she said.

"You were named after a good and noble man," Mamu said.

"Yes, the man who threw out the man who'd saved him—and you."

"That was not your grandfather's intention. He made a mistake."

"Oh, so that's what it was."

"My first Robert was a kind, brilliant, imaginative, loving man, the way my second Robert is. Yes, he made a mistake. He was human, like the rest of us."

"Why not Paul? Why didn't I get his name?"

"Because he may be alive. We are hoping he is alive."

"And what about Raoul?"

"Raoul too. We pray he is alive. He would be a saint to us, if we had saints." She sighed. "You have the chance to redeem the name Robert. Your grandfather would have given anything to have Paul back, and he would have given anything to have met you. He would have cherished you, you know. You look like him. You have much of his character. We must have divined something when we named you."

Music came from the other room. It was Medea singing again. My father and great-aunt were back. Hermina had brought bags filled with clothing for Attila and me. She'd even bought us proper suitcases to carry our new things in.

FIFTEEN

WE ALL MET IN the kitchen, but my brother was missing. My mother searched the house for him. I found him in the shed. It was obvious he'd been crying. When I opened the door, he was sitting on top of the black trunk. "Hello, my fine Hungarian boy," he said. I knew this was the best he could do for now.

The late morning sun beamed in the window, turning him into a glowhead. His cheeks were shiny with tears. I wanted to hug him, but that would have been going too far. I'd never seen my brother this way. Granted, I had shared only 9.8 of his 13.7 years, really just 71.5 percent of his life, but I had never seen him so moved. In fact, since I was not present when our great-aunt sang "Pur ti miro," I'd never seen him moved at all.

"I found a diary," he said.

"In the trunk?"

He pulled a leather-bound notebook out from under himself. "I found it before."

"Before what?"

"Before you were in here."

"And you kept it from me?"

He didn't answer. We were even now, even if he didn't know it. He opened the diary to a page he'd marked, and he read out loud again.

7 November 1951

I didn't think there could be much surprise left for me in the world, and yet there is. Colonel Josef Dortmund showed up at Ede's office today! If he had not directly been my tormentor, he felt responsible for it. Here he was, complaining of a stomach ailment and asking Ede to help him, the only doctor he trusted. The Dortmunds are living in Paris now! They were originally Volksdeutsche *from Alsace, living on the French side, and his wife's family is French. Now they have moved to Paris! He spent three years in prison for his crimes. We have been invited to visit with them when Colonel Dortmund gets better. They live over on rue Guy de Maupassant, number 21. He gave the address to my Ede freely. Imagine it!—We could now be friends. Take a gâteau to their house, sit and smile and have tea and cake. I would, of course, wear my elegant gloves.*

My Ede will do his duty and help the man if he can. They are both men of duty.—Ede will do his duty, just as Dortmund was doing his.

My brother looked up from his book. "This man hurt our family," he said. "I don't know how. I searched earlier in the diary, but there's no hint."

I was about to tell Attila, but I was worried about how he'd react, and in any case, he didn't give me time. "It's the Second Coming," he said. "Do you see it?"

I took a step back. "Yes, I do. I mean no, I don't. I'm very young."

"I want you to listen now," he said. "I want to show you the Statue Graveyard in living Technicolor."

My brother reached behind him and pulled out an army helmet. With a grunt, he plopped it onto his head. "Heavy," he said. He turned his head one way and the other, modeling it for me. It had a golden eagle on its side, standing on the same wheel with the bent spokes, the swastika. "The helmet was in the trunk," Attila said. "The question is how Uncle Ede and Aunt Hermina came to have it."

"Maybe they saved the man's life," I said. "The helmet wearer's life."

"Yes, the helmet wearer's life—what a bright little seedling you are. Do you think they spent more time with Colonel Dortmund than we know? Do you think their oppressor would show up at Uncle Ede's office if he didn't feel safe?"

The helmet was too big for my brother's head. He kept adjusting some straps inside until finally it sat just right, if a little heavily, on his head. He began his speech again. "Everyone is searching for the meaning of life. We belong to certain categories, like Rock, Bird, Human, but it is only humans who choose subcategories to divide themselves into. Pigeons and carp don't do that. Adam and Eve lived in a very good place, very, very good. But part of the original plan of creation was that they would choose to fall. Oh, yes." My brother held up his index finger. "Oh, yes. The Lord saw it coming. He is omniscient. If everything is good, how can God's special creatures choose him? They don't know any better. So he sent along the serpent and said unto it, 'You make sure they eat the fruit of the tree of the knowledge of good and evil.' And on that day, we became choosers. Eve chose the fruit. Adam chose Eve. Sometimes we're good at it, sometimes not." My brother reached behind him and then raised his *Gott mit Uns* belt buckle to his eye. "'God with us,' it means. Mamu told me."

"You showed her the buckle."

"No, I just asked her what it meant. 'God with us.' So you see, you've found God after all." He slapped the side of his helmet. "You have found him again, far from the Garden, and now you're able to say, 'I am the greatest.' We all want to say it, but to be the greatest implies that someone else is not so great. To this person I award a shitty cloth star." My brother held up the cloth Star of David and spoke to it. He had a number of objects behind him on the lid of the trunk. "You are vermin," he said to the star, "and we must get a special pesticide to eradicate you." He flung the star across the room.

I went to get it. I wanted to hold it. I took a seat on the footstool. "So where does that leave us?" he asked. I shrugged my shoulders. "It brings us to the heart of the matter," he said, "that's where. Give me your sleeve. I want to wipe my nose."

"I'll give you the back of my underpants."

He ran the palm of his hand under his nose and up his cheek. A cloud passed over the sun, graying the room, giving it drama. "You see," my brother said. He was pointing to the window. "The eye of heaven blinked. It is here, my slovenly boy, that things fall apart. Bear with me."

"Who else am I going to bear with?"

"Someone says, 'I am the greatest,' and mows down what is in his path, since everything and everyone else must be less than the greatest. It is the only thing that makes sense. Then a second group comes along and says, 'No, you are not the greatest,' and this second group pushes back. Some from this second group secretly want to be the greatest too, and they want to prove it by beating the first group. There is a third group, sensible and orderly, and they just want to go on with their lives, make the best of what they have, do whatever good they can for themselves and others, carry on, carry on, carry on, until they inherit the earth. This group contains *our* grandfather Robert."

I was pleased to hear him say "our grandfather." "He meant no harm," I put in.

"No, he meant no harm. Usually. But this once he lost his head. He wanted to be the bigger man, or as big, just once. People in this group mean no harm, even if they cause some. Many of the people we know are in this group, maybe we are too. Right?"

"Right. But maybe you're not. Maybe you're slightly disturbed."

He ignored me. He said, "Then there is a fourth group, a few people who say no to the ones who think they are the greatest. They risk their own lives and find the only meaning they can in doing so. They fight to help their peers, help them and save them, put themselves in harm's way to do so. Our own Paul Beck is a member of this group. Hitler's resisters even in his own country are in this group. They lost their heads in resisting; then they lost their actual heads."

"What about Raoul Wallenberg?"

"And then there's Raoul Wallenberg. Raoul belongs to his own group. Sometimes it's not even a group, just a solitary soul. This is the fifth group, the apex. They come out of nowhere, or somewhere, the Garden of Eden—they can still smell the Garden of Eden—and they know what it takes to get us back there. They have no other reason to help or even save people other than that scent, that sense of the possibility of things. Raoul is the Second Coming. Or Raoul is the First Coming, depending on who it is you're talking to, and he is the one foreseen by Isaiah. How else is he going to show up? Dressed in a toga? On a beam of light? No. He is a thin, balding young Swede who shows up in Budapest wanting to do good and is smart enough to figure out how to do it. Then one day he is taken away for his efforts, not from the Via Dolorosa, not even from Andrassy Avenue, but from a shitty street in Debrecen. And poof, he's gone."

"When do you have these thoughts?" I asked him.

"Can you think things while you're swinging through the trees?"

My brother cleared his throat and wiped his cheeks and nose on his sleeve, a bold move, since he liked to keep his shirts neat and clean.

"Maybe it was the tree and the flowers," I said.

"What was, my dim-witted boy?" He sniffled.

"What if it wasn't the Lord at all who expelled Adam and Eve from the Garden? Maybe it wasn't enough for them to slosh around among the flowers. You can have too many flowers," I said.

"Yes." My brother pointed at me. "Yes, you can have too many flowers. Where is Noseboy when we need him?"

"So maybe it was the flowers," I said.

"Yes," my brother said. He was still pointing at me, pointing at the air. He started shouting. "The flowers saw a chance in Adam and Eve, and yes, you have it—you can have too many flowers, too much perfume. They saw a chance with the humans. They could spread the flowers outside the Garden. They could spread the flowers all over the world. The flowers rose up against them to cast them out of paradise. They thrust up their pink lady dicks with the seeds standing out of them. 'Take us,' they said. 'Let us rub up against you and leave our essence on you, so you can scatter us, so your wicked children can plant garden after garden all over the world. We'll color your planet. We'll sweeten your planet, and if you don't like color or sweetness, we have no use for you.' And so they went forth, Adam and Eve and their wicked children, and their wicked children after them—or after the one, to be precise—and the joke was on them because of the cycle of things, my fawn-eyed boy. You spend the rest of eternity trying to get back to the Garden. You have a live electrical wire that drives you on, drives you toward that golden land, in whatever feeble or misguided or half-witted way you think you can make it. Yes, a spark, a live wire."

My brother was standing now, quite straight and tall. I said, "I think yours is more live than other people's wires, until it's switched off."

"We have a job to do," he said, ignoring me. "If we don't do something while Paul might still be alive, we'll be banning him a second time from our lives."

"What if he doesn't want us to find him? What if he's had enough of us? It's been more than ten years."

"We have to find him, maybe even Raoul after him, with Paul's help. We wouldn't be here, still roaming among the grasses and rocks, if they hadn't come along. This is history we're talking about, the making of history. History isn't finished."

He took off his helmet, turned toward the trunk, and then, with a flourish, spun around again. A gun had appeared in his hand—an impressive one.

I leapt to my feet. "Where did you get that?"

The door of the shed opened. My brother shoved the gun behind him. Our mother and grandmother were standing there. "What are you two doing in here?" asked our mother. Then she noticed some of the items on the lid of the trunk. "Oh, no."

"We have to find Paul and Raoul and Colonel Dort-mund," Attila announced.

Our mother gasped. "What are you saying?"

Mamu was calmer. "Come and eat breakfast," she said. "You still haven't had breakfast."

"We can't delay." My brother looked at me. His fury fumes beat their wings around me until I would have to rise with him or against him. There was no middle ground.

"We'll have breakfast," our grandmother said. "That long we can delay."

Babette was whipping up a fresh batch of omelets flecked with mushrooms. Our mother and grandmother sat with us. Our father was in the room that had been given to our parents, and Hermina was playing Handel in the solarium. I could hardly hear the music—my father had probably asked her to keep it down—but I could hear her voice, singing along with the record.

"My sister's replacing all my records," our grandmother said, "the ones that were lost and even the ones I left be-hind at home. She'll be shipping them to us, wherever we end up." She sighed. I pictured the night my father had broken some of her records, the night Judit died. It seemed far away and long ago. Our mother put her hand over our grandmother's.

Babette smiled at each of us in turn as she brought us our eggs. My brother was brooding. He didn't even take notice of Babette, much less breathe in the cream of her skin. Nor did he ask a single question of anyone. He didn't roll out his thesis about mushrooms, even though we were eating some. He didn't ask, "How many people, through trial and error, do you suppose, consumed mushrooms and then died before we realized which ones we could eat and which ones we couldn't?" He didn't say, "Since word traveled poorly in the first mushroom-eating days, in how many tribes, hamlets, or labyrinths of caves did bad-mushroom eating occur before the news spread and a conclusion could be drawn and then relayed back throughout the land? Also, was the mushroom an attractive item to consume compared to an orange or an apple, never mind a peach, even though biting into the first peach must have been a little like biting into a juicy cardigan?"

Babette poured each of us a glass of milk. She swooped around my brother's shoulder to pour, resting there too long, I thought. I was more than a little jealous. This was the first time in a long time that I had an inkling of a new category to be added to Fluttering Things and Glowheads, and to be called Creamy Goodness.

Yet my brother was unmoved. A butterfly of light fluttered on his face as he drank. We were all waiting for something out of him. But all he did was stare down at his plate, picking with his fork at the lacy edge of his egg.

Our father came into the kitchen just as my brother and I were finishing. The music stopped, and Hermina joined us too. Her curved pink hands were naked in the daylight. She had bought my brother and me matching sailor outfits, complete with caps, and she presented them to us now. My brother looked grimly at his outfit and wouldn't take it.

I put on my sailor's cap to make Hermina feel better.

Babette cleared away our plates and glasses as she smiled broadly at us all and said something sweet-sounding in French.

"Boys, just because we're refugees," our father said, "doesn't mean we can't be tourists too. We are privileged, thanks to our generous relative. She has agreed to take us to see some of Paris's legendary sights."

Aunt Hermina clapped her hands together, but instead they clopped, on account of their hollowed-out shape.

Attila stood up, faced her, and said, "We have to find Paul. Robert and I know what happened. We know everything. We can't wait. We have work to do."

A storm formed behind my father's eyes. It was a look he shared with Attila. "How do you know?" He spoke calmly. He looked at the women. "It's been more than a decade," he went on. "We have tried, believe me. We don't know what happened to the dear man, but if he ever reappeared I'd give him anything he asked for, anything I could, not that we have much anymore."

"He's not just going to show up after all this time," Attila said and slapped his side. "Especially after what happened. We have to search for him."

Our father took Attila's shoulders in his grip. "You have to forget Paul Beck," he said. "Paul is trouble. Wallenberg was trouble, and Paul might have followed him."

Attila shrugged free. He was shaking. "So you agree with that man on the bus. Is that what you're saying, Father? That Paul was a menace? Raoul Wallenberg was a menace?"

"Of course I'm not saying that."

"Paul's not trouble," Attila said. "He stood in the way of trouble, like Raoul."

Hermina clopped her hands together again. "But Paul *was* trouble. Thank God for his trouble, that darling man."

"Yes," our father said. "Of course, Paul stood in the way of trouble." He was speaking calmly. "Paul needed to assert himself. He needed to be who he was. And my father, your grandfather, needed to be who he was, to assert himself, to be the head of his household and assert what he thought was right. That's all. We were past considerations of saviors—who was one and who wasn't. Saviors often go unappreciated. It's the nature of the calling." Everyone stared at our father, but no one spoke. "Now, here's what we are going to do today," he said, taking hold of my brother again. "We are going into Paris to see one of the great European wonders. There is no other city like it. I don't know when we'll be back here. Certainly I will not be back."

Looking straight into our father's eyes, Attila said, "Do you think it's all right just to drop your cousin from your thoughts? I'm not talking about Raoul Wallenberg or Jesus Christ. I'm talking about Paul. He saved us. Without him we wouldn't even be having this conversation right now. The least we can do is find out what happened to him. We can't be cowards now."

"I'm sorry to have disappointed you," our father said with a steely evenness in his voice. "No one questions your suitability as a child. Why do you question mine as a parent?"

200

"What?" Attila asked, and our father was about to answer, but our mother stepped between them. My brother turned and marched off to our room. My father had a murderous look. I thought of Medea and quickly followed my brother.

Our mother brought our sailors' suits to us. She did this right away, too soon. She said gently, "Attila."

"Please!" he snapped, and she withdrew.

I got into my suit, including the cap, as my brother stared out the library window. He wouldn't look at me or answer me, and when I put my hand on his shoulder, he brushed it away. After quite some time, I heard music again, not a record this time, but our great-aunt, singing softly down the hall in the solarium. I wanted to please her with my outfit, so I made my way down. She was swaying as before, hugging her shoulders with the claws of her hands, and dancing with herself. I walked boldly in. She noticed the outfit and smiled and took me in her arms to join in her swaying. My cap fell off.

"What is it?" I asked, but she kept singing, smoothing the hair at the back of my head. I was very hot. The song was quiet and seemed, at moments, to stand still, the notes hanging there in the quiet.

"It is by Rameau. *Castor et Pollux,*" my great-aunt said. *Tristes apprêts, pâles flambeaux . . .*

She sang the lyrics to the aria, singing out the story to me as we danced. "Sad finish, pale flames," she translated. "They're brothers."

"Who are?"

"Castor and Pollux. They're brothers from ancient

Greece," she sang. "But they're different in one important way. They have the same mother. Her name is Leda. But Castor's father is a person, a human, while Pollux's father is Zeus."

"The god," I said.

"Yes, the god of gods." Hermina stopped singing. She was speaking now, too close to my ear, I felt, as we continued to dance, and she held me with her bird hands. "Zeus appears to Leda in the form of a swan and—" Hermina paused. "They unite," she said.

"With the swan?" I tried to pull back, but my great-aunt returned to her singing, the same haunting tune. "Why was it a swan? Why wasn't it a serpent or a lion or a wolf, possibly?"

"No, he is a swan, but a swan infused with the power and sorcery of Zeus. After a time, Leda lays an egg from which the brothers hatch.

"One day on a battlefield, Castor is slain. Pollux lifts up his lifeless brother, holds him up to heaven, shakes the body, loose as a skeleton already. Zeus smiles down upon them, and do you know what Zeus does for the two brothers?" I shook my head. "Zeus raises the two brothers to the heavens in the form of the constellation Gemini."

"Gemini! I know the brothers. I *know* that constellation. And Castor and Pollux are the brightest stars in it!"

"I thank you," my great-aunt said, "for putting on the sailor suit."

I blushed as if I had been exposed, and she sang the soothing notes of the song again. I was moved by the song even more this second time. "I love this song," I said, "those notes, how they go together, as if they've always been together."

My great-aunt was delighted with my remark but paused before answering me. She was still humming, singing some words.

Then she said, "Those notes, those holy notes." She put both hands on her heart. And she sang once more and hummed.

"Aunt Hermina," I said, after another moment, and I did so as warmly as I could, "why do you sing so many songs about dead children?"

She stopped singing. She sat down on a chair and covered her mouth with the bowls of her hands. "Oh," she whispered. And then she was about to say something else but didn't. She looked distracted. I didn't know what else to say either. I bent down to hug my great-aunt but couldn't manage it. She was slumped over a bit, not in hugging mode, so I slowly backed out of the solarium instead.

I returned to the library and sat on my bed. My brother was still there, his back to me, busy with things on the desk. But after a long time, he finally broke the terrible silence. He'd been studying maps he'd found in the desk drawers and turned to see if I wanted to go into the city, as our father had promised.

"Yes," I said, very happy about the change in his mood.

He went out to the salon to ask our mother to ask our father if he was still willing to take us. Our father said he was not.

"But you have to," she told him.

"I do not."

"Yes, my darling," our grandmother said. "You have to. These are your boys, and they have a chance to see Paris, and we cannot leave until they do."

Just as he relented, someone banged at the front door quite hard and then banged again. It sounded like a fist. Aunt Hermina came out of the solarium, but Babette was ahead of her. We all followed. Babette opened the door with a smile.

Two burly men dressed in suits and trench coats stood there, blocking out the light. They asked for my parents by name: "Simon Beck, Lili Beck." But when Hermina asked in French what they wanted, we realized the men were not French. They were Russian. They said something in Russian, and each took one of my parents by the arm. Attila threw himself at them, but one of the men swatted him away. My brother went flying against the wall and crumpled to the floor. Our mother screamed, but they pulled a burlap hood over her head and another over our father's head. They hustled our parents out to a waiting car and sped away.

SIXTEEN

"WHERE ARE THEY TAKING THEM?" I asked. I was sob-
bing, gasping for air. I was thinking about where the
German officers had taken our Aunt Hermina and
Uncle Ede.

My brother was out cold on the floor. He had a cut
over his eye, and Babette ran to get something for him.
My grandmother and great-aunt, the calm and calming
sisters, looked ready to pull at each other, to pluck out
feathers if they had any.

For a moment, only Babette seemed to know what
to do. She arrived with a linen towel to hold over my
brother's eye while she cradled his head in her lap.

Hermina seemed to want to rake her own face with
her hands. "I'll call a doctor," she said. She said something else to Babette, in French, and Babette agreed. "I
know the chief of police," Hermina said. "I'll call him.

We'll go straight to him. We'll get your parents back. But first the doctor."

Mamu, Babette, and I moved Attila into the library and laid him down on his bed. He groaned but didn't open his eyes. One eyelid had already swollen. Babette switched on the lamp above his head and kissed him on the forehead. She kissed me too, and she had me hold the cloth while she went to get other things.

I stared at my brother and whispered his name, but he didn't answer. Then I barked his name, but he didn't even flinch. On the desk there were maps of France and Paris, along with a French-Hungarian dictionary. I pulled the chair back from the desk; underneath it Attila had stashed the German helmet from the shed, the war helmet with the eagle and the swastika. Inside it were the flashlight and the pistol.

It came over me in a wave that our parents were gone. What if they were gone for good? What if Attila was going now too? I had to suck back a new round of sobbing, but in its place I uncorked a flood of hiccuping. I'd be an orphan. I'd be parentless, brotherless. Yes, I'd still be grandmotherful and auntful, but it was too much to consider all at once. Not one of the things that was happening so quickly seemed right or earned or natural. I was hoping we had sidestepped history by taking this detour into France, but I guess I was wrong. It probably would not have suited my brother, in any case, to sidestep history. If he had seen it looking the other way, he would have redirected its focus back on us in a hurry.

I turned to him again. There he lay still in the lamplight, shiny, pink, appled up for the New World—he made no sense this way. He breathed in thinly and breathed out through the reeds of his throat. The books around us seemed to huddle in a conference over him, like a secret society. I gently pried open his unharmed eyelid—he had the dead glass look of the hanging man. I let the lid fall. I felt myself salting up again. There were bad omens floating in the air, soap bubbles of them, and I wanted to pop them. I wished my great-aunt would sing. I wished she would put on some music, something to distract me, to wake my brother, to lure an angel to slip in through the window.

That was exactly what we needed. In what creature other than an angel did fluttering things, glowheads, and creamy goodness overlap? She'd be a wonder. My brother would spring straight up in bed if he saw her. He'd feed off her. She'd be humming a melody for all the ages, but my brother would want to know first why she looked like us. Why was she an extra-beautiful version of ourselves? Why did she have hair? Did she have hair in the other places too? In other words, was she almost entirely like us? Did she have internal organs or just airy ones, celestial ones? Did she have a scent, or was it something only Noseboy could detect? Never mind the wings. He would be pawing them like mad. He'd ask if they were designed only for shuttling up and down, or for flying to and fro as well, the way a bird does. She wouldn't need to cruise like a gull, surely, or swoop like a hawk after spying the movement of a field mouse in the grass. What would be the point of it? Attila would inspect her closely, wanting to know how the wings attached to the back, wanting to pluck out a feather, keep one for later study, but then find that he couldn't, that these were not bird feathers but something more durable—dateless feathers, feathers without end, wings without equal, something crystalline rather than feathery. He'd be touching the angel as she hummed, handling her overly, admiring her angelic boobs. What would an angel's boobs be for except to admire? He would want to know if she was part of the cycle of things. Was she the afterlife of sheep or something more, a dead soldier in a field, the brass buttons on his coat, a toppled statue, or the light of an old star? What about numerals, the parts of speech—adjectives, adverbs, pronouns? And what about events? Could you throw a whole event into the makeup of an angel— the storming of the Bastille, the coronation of the Emperor Franz Josef, the first flight of the *Hindenburg,* the discovery of penicillin? How about events that had not yet happened to go with the timeless wings and airy organs—relocating Eden, having a picnic on Mars? Could you not—*should* you not—blend these all together in an angel so that she could carry down a melody from heaven for you to play?

My grandmother looked in on us. She kissed my brother and inspected his swollen eye. It was his right eye, the eye he most often closed to the sun. And then she sat with me on my bed to stare at him. For a giddy moment I wondered if my brother had just gone to sleep in an instant, the way he always did.

My grandmother held my hand, and a chill came over

me. "I'm scared," I told her. She was silent. She was having trouble looking at me. I realized she wanted to say she was scared too, but she couldn't. She wasn't supposed to. What a bind she was in. I could wallow and wail in my sadness and fear if I wanted to—but she couldn't.

The doctor came to examine my brother. He was Hungarian, a friend of the family. All of us were in the room when another call came from the police to say that our grandmother and great-aunt could meet with the authorities at the station. The doctor had heard what happened and said he knew a member of the French National Assembly, if we needed him. He bandaged up my brother's cut. He then lifted Attila's eyelids, and his blue eyes still had the dead glass look in them. I felt I might get sick. I covered my mouth. The doctor said we'd have to keep an eye on him, but he didn't say what we might or might not see. He also told us that Attila might wake up or he might stay down, depending—but he didn't say what it depended on. He said he'd be back first thing the next morning and was gone.

Babette covered Attila's forehead next to the bandage with a wet cloth and kissed him repeatedly just where the cloth met the forehead, as though she wanted to suck away the harm.

Hermina's hands were trembling. She asked my grandmother to accompany her to the police—she'd feel better if the two of them could go together, she said. Babette was very capable of looking after us boys.

Babette smiled and said something to my brother in French as she held her place beside him and went on dabbing his forehead, careful to avoid the dressing beside the eye.

A few minutes after my grandmother and great-aunt were gone, Babette stretched out beside my brother on his bed and cradled his head in her arm. I stood and watched, enthralled. She signaled for me to join them. Attila had the bigger of the two daybeds in the room, but with three people in it I guessed we'd be cramped. She beckoned to me, though, and beckoned some more, smiling all the while, so I squeezed in on the opposite side and wedged my head in the other warm cradle.

A blue vapor rose in the room, blue being the color of creamy goodness in its gaseous state. I dozed off, or swooned, more likely. Whether it was a minute or an hour later I don't know, but I was wakened by a slurping sound and turned to find my brother sucking like mad on Babette's white neck. His eyes were still closed—had they ever opened?—and now he rubbed her stomach lightly before rising and taking the shape of her covered breast in his hand. His hand was trembling. I didn't dare move, didn't dare let on that I was conscious. Was my brother conscious? Was Babette? Everyone's eyes, even mine some of the time, were closed in the lamplight. Babette had a love bite on her white neck as sharp as a tattoo, a purple carnation, possibly, the petals etched out by Attila's teeth.

My brother looked at me now through the warm cut of his eye. Babette's plump breast, the one nearest my brother, was out, taking in the light. My brother latched on to the thick nipple. Babette unleashed her second breast and offered it to me. She was a human pudding. I took the warm bud in my mouth. Babette made a French sound. The current running through me from the base of my spine told me that this moment would enter the boiler room of my memory, that even if there were ten of me, this memory would store enough fuel to last each of us a thousand years. I glanced over the soft creamy terrain at my brother. Babette's flesh seemed to give off light, empurpled only by the shadows of our heads. I was sucking so hard that I thought I would bring forth milk.

If ever there was a time to review creation, this was it. Was that paradise up ahead? We could return to Eden. We could start again with darkness and light, the water and the land and air and fire, the sun and the moon, yellow and silver. But after that? Ban the serpent. Let there be fruit but no tree of the knowledge of good and evil. What good was it? What was wrong with staying stupid? Stupid was better than smart, if smart led to killing. We could then love the Lord as stupid people who loved him without thinking. After all, lots of stupid people loved him now.

Babette unlatched each of us and sat up fully. She kissed my brother on the forehead and smiled, seeing that she had cured him. And then she hovered over me too. I put forward my muscled lips for her soft ones, but she kissed me on the forehead as well. She got up, rearranged and covered herself, then switched off the lamp and walked lightly out, pulling all the warmth with her as she floated on air and then was gone.

★   ★   ★

"We have to go now," my brother said to me in the darkness. He sounded drunk.

I switched the lamp back on. "Where?"

It was then that the wave rolled over me again. My mother was gone. My father too. But the wave always brought my mother first. How could they throw a burlap sack over light that bright? Surely she would smile and, seeing the light, they would let her go.

"Come, my boy," he said. "We have much to do."

"Why are you talking like this?" I felt feverish.

Attila was already getting up and fidgeting, checking his bandage, looking under the desk for the helmet. "Didn't you hear, or was I talking to myself? Colonel Dortmund lives in Paris now."

"What are you talking about?" I looked at my brother's bandaged head.

"And they have them," he said. "Or weren't you paying attention to that either?"

"Who has them? What are you saying?"

"The Russians. They kidnapped Raoul Wallenberg, and now they want Paul too. They must think our parents can lead them to Paul."

"But they can't."

"They won't believe them. They'll question them. They may even hurt them. The question is why they didn't come for them in Budapest. Maybe Paul—wherever he is—has been pushing for Wallenberg's release, and now the Russians want to find him and shut him up."

"What can we do? Where would they be?"

"Where would you have taken them?"

"I don't know," I said. "I've never taken people."

My brother grabbed hold of my shoulders. "They've taken them somewhere secret. They can't take them to the police stations. They're *Russian.* They must have gone underground." Paris has a sewer system running underneath the whole of the city, he said. *Les égouts de Paris,* it's called. He was getting out the map he'd been studying, together with the dictionary. "We have to find them," Attila said and claimed to know of an entrance near a bridge named the Pont de l'Alma.

"But how can you know that? How did you find out?"

"Les Misérables."

"What?"

"A novel, by Victor Hugo." He was pacing again, all the while adjusting his bandage. He started proclaiming. "Hugo called the sewers 'the conscience of the city,'" Attila said.

"Is Tarzan in the novel?"

"No," he barked.

"Whisper to me," I told him. *"Whisper."*

My brother took a deep breath. "Let's sneak out the back," he said, "where the shed is. We can't let Babette see us."

And there was all this French coming out of my brother's mouth now—the rue Guy de Maupassant and the Pont de l'Alma. "We won't be seeing beautiful Paris," he said, "the Eiffel Tower and the *Mona Lisa* and the

Arc de Triomphe. We'll be seeing ugly Paris. But first Colonel Dortmund."

"What about the men who came here? Are we going to beat them up?" And now my heart was pounding.

My brother pulled the gun from underneath the desk and put on the helmet. He shone the flashlight in my face. "I'll do the dirty work. Please, leave it to me. I can go alone, except I'll need you to hold the flashlight for questioning."

"Questioning," I repeated aloud. "Will I need something? A helmet or a sword or anything?"

"You will have the flashlight. You'll light up things."

He took out notepaper from the desk as well as an impressive black fountain pen. He wrote something on the paper: 6 rue Père Goriot. He said, "This is Aunt Hermina's address. Have it with you, in case."

"In case of what?"

"In case we get separated."

"I'll memorize it."

"They won't understand you when you say it, no matter how hard you try. Just keep the note."

I shoved the paper into my pocket. Attila took off the helmet and put it back on, adjusting it around the bandage, tucking the bandage under the strap. The helmet was much too big for him, but he did something more with the strap to make it fit. Though he looked ridiculous, the helmet seemed to give him courage. A hard look came over him.

"We have to be very quiet now, my cloven-hoofed boy," he said.

214

Before we made our way to the back, my brother pulled me in the opposite direction, toward our great-aunt's bedroom. When we were inside, he closed the door behind us and switched on the light, a pink chandelier with floral stems, leaves, and petals holding the bulbs. The theme was repeated on the bedposts. They seemed alive, seemed to move when you half looked away from them.

The cream dressing table had blond wooden arms on it. The hands at the ends of the arms were held up, like greeting hands, waving hands, and each was wearing a long glove of a different color—pale green, pale yellow, pale blue. The gloved hands cast dramatic shadows on the wall.

Who made those wooden hands for Hermina? Did she look at them in the night or the half-light before waking and imagine her own hands whole? Pink lady hands rather than bird hands?

I kept picturing her out there in the cold, hanging. How can you hang out a singer in the cold by her fingertips, like hanging a nightingale? How about hanging someone by the fingertips who's not a singer, who's tone deaf? Or someone who only *likes* music? Or someone who *doesn't* like music at all? It was hard to think of a person suitable for hanging by the fingertips.

My brother was staring at the same table. "There," Attila said.

"The hands?" I said.

"Yes. It's an old trick of the ladies."

We approached the table, and he felt each of the fingers.

"Wait," he said. He opened the only drawer, where other gloves lay sleeping and handless. He took out several, pulled on one pair after another, then clanged his helmet with a fist.

"What are you doing?" I asked.

"We need some French money. Mamu keeps money in the fingers of her gloves, or she did back home. Mother too. Where do you think I got extra cash when I needed it?"

"Why don't we ask Babette?"

"Because she can't know we're leaving, my baby assailant. I thought that part was clear."

"Very little of this is clear."

My brother threw the gloves back in the drawer. What I wanted in the worst way was to steal a pair of the waving wooden hands themselves. I don't know why. I would not have bragged about them or shown them to friends. I just wanted them to look at when no one else was around. I wanted to measure them to see if they would fit into my bag or maybe the small new suitcase Hermina had bought me.

But Attila said it was time to go. He adjusted his helmet. I had the flashlight. He had the gun.

We got outside as quietly as we could and waited to see if any sounds came from inside the town house before we moved on. Ragged clouds curtained over the moon, but there was still enough moonlight to see the shed. We headed out to rue Père Goriot and began our walk toward the concentrated lights of Paris.

Each time a car passed, we turned to see if it was a taxi.

One did approach, but it zoomed by, possibly because the driver caught sight of my brother's helmet. A few minutes later another slowed and then sped up again. When the next taxi turned the corner in our direction, Attila leapt into the road in front of it. He aimed his gun at the windshield. The car screeched to a halt. Its engine even cut out.

"*Vingt-et-un* rue Guy de Maupassant," my brother said to the closed window.

The man was trying to restart the engine. My brother put his hand on the rear door handle.

"What are you doing?" I asked. I gripped his arm, the one holding the gun.

"Just watch me," he said.

The driver was as terrified as I was.

We got in. "*Vingt-et-un* rue Guy de Maupassant," Attila said more fiercely. He pointed the gun at the back of the man's head. The driver screeched away even before we were settled in our seats.

I stared at my brother, the hard look of him, and for a single moment, I felt safe.

Paris was as beautiful as everyone said, with its river and its elegant buildings, each like an overgrown sculpture. Its lights were soft and amber like Hermina's. They were like night embers, but we tore by them all, smearing the light.

When we arrived, the driver said something we couldn't understand. But Attila, being Attila, now wanted advice from the man. He handed me the gun, unfolded his map, and seemed to be asking how we could get from the rue Guy de Maupassant to the Pont de l'Alma. It turned out it was right around the corner.

"Just as I thought," Attila said to me.

I stared at my brother. "Who *are* you?" I said.

He snatched the gun back, and we got out. The car tore away even before I'd closed the door behind me.

We walked for only a couple of minutes before we arrived at a squat brownstone building right on the corner. We had to climb over a low wrought-iron fence and edge along a flower bed to get to the front. The town house was guarded by an impressive elm tree. It had tall windows, and lights were on inside. Attila and I crept toward a lighted window, crunching over some fallen leaves. Inside, a man sat in a leather chair reading a book.

"Colonel Josef Dortmund," my brother whispered.

A trim middle-aged woman came in and set a cup of tea by the man's side. Then a boy with hair as blond as Attila's but a couple of years older looked into the room and said something to the man and woman, which caused them both to answer and shake their heads. The boy slapped at the door frame and marched away. He could have passed for Attila's brother more easily than I did.

My brother aimed the gun at the window. "What are you doing?" I whispered.

"Exacting revenge."

"You don't even know what he did."

"He hurt us."

"So you're executing him now?"

"No—just scaring him," he said and fired the gun

through the window. The man's lamp shattered as well as the window itself, of course. Shouting and scrambling came from inside.

"Let's go!" my brother said, and he pinched my upper arm hard. We leapt over the fence and raced off. "This way," he said, yanking me down an alley and over onto another avenue.

My legs had noodled over. I could barely stand. I braced myself against a building, but the sound of a door closing inside caused us to rush off again.

"There it is!" Attila said, pointing with his gun. "The Pont de l'Alma!" And he laughed! He actually laughed.

We crossed another street, and then the stench hit us.

If you are ever searching for the a-hole of the world, search no further. My brother and I found it in Paris, by the Pont de l'Alma. There were houses all around it, and a romantic bridge. But what sort of romance was possible as lovers strolled over this bridge holding hands or went to their beds in the homes nearby? I bet there were very few babies made in this neighborhood.

I was gasping, trying to breathe right. The gate to the sewers was unlocked but clanged and squealed impressively as we pulled it open. We clumped down the iron spiral stairs, expecting to encounter rats and criminals and the abductors of our parents. Nothing and no one would have surprised me.

But the stench, the intensity of it. When we reached the bottom, we had to stop. We had to pause to admire the dark river glubbing by, this wonder of the world. Lights down below lit up everything the city had expelled from the land above: leftover cabbage soup, even *digested* cabbage soup, fingernails and toenails, an earring, the nightly bathwater, a razor blade with a bit of face still stuck to it, cigar butts, the flow of a bad stomach, the flow of a good one, a gold wedding band, bones, knives, guns, vomit, dead goldfish, live mollies, hairs— blond, brunette, gray, auburn, true black, dyed black, dyed blond, dyed red—hairs by the millions and trillions, short hairs, long ones, curly ones, eyelashes, a mother-of-pearl button— *What would Noseboy say? Was this where Noseboys came to die?*—marzipan monkeys, a guitar pick, brown milk, teeth, handkerchiefs, a clarinet reed, a clarinet, creamy goodness, twenty thousand francs rolled up in the fingers of a long glove once white, possibly, red wine, white wine, clear water, juicy plums, red beets— the browning over of everything—pieces of salmon, petits fours, turnips, bits of toothpaste, the bleeding from gums, the tip of the finger of a glowhead, a gold watch chain, two pages of a book, thoughts of you washed off a face, a stillborn, a lapis lazuli to bring out your eyes, the testicle sweat of a wrestler, the testicles of a bloodhound, the spit of opinions, tens of thousands of trillions of Xs and Ys wiggling their way to battle.

"We have found the river of Hades, the river of the underworld," my brother said.

A bat flew through, and then, as if on cue, a rat scrambled by, creatures traveling the sky and ground of this underworld in search of things they could use to survive. Was everything down here in the sewers expelled from somewhere else? Was it possible there were also splendid beings living here, or were even the splendid beings fallen versions of themselves?

You felt as if you wanted a mighty wind to blow through, a driving rain. My brother suddenly held his head, held his helmet, actually. He had a strange look in his eyes. I didn't need my flashlight to see that they were bloodshot. I shined the light all around us and at the pipes emptying into Shit River, trickling, gurgling, flowing out to the Seine to tint the ocean.

All at once out of the far darkness came a yelp. A girl no older than I was, dressed only in a drab night-gown, flew at us. She grabbed on to Attila for a second. Her black hair was wild and her face crazed, even in the dim light. She couldn't speak or catch her breath. Sirens sounded in her all the way down to her bare feet.

We quickly knew the cause. An even wilder man, who could have passed for Rasputin, crashed into us and clutched the girl by the neck just as she let go of my brother. I thought we were finished, all of us. I was para-lyzed.

But Attila was not. He flashed his gun, and the girl squirmed out of the man's grasp and flung herself at me, clinging, the way a cat might, all needles and softness and panting heart. Attila aimed the gun straight at the bearded man's face and barked at him in Hungarian to let the girl go. The wildness shifted in the man's eyes. I joined the assault with the beam of my flashlight, the girl took off, and, with a single brute shove, my brother top-pled the man into the River Kaka.

"Let's go," Attila said to me. "Now!"

For a moment I couldn't move, watching the girl go. I was in love with her already. I'd fallen for her as quickly as I'd fallen for Babette.

Rasputin thrashed to the edge, left a wet handprint on the brick.

"Let's go!" my brother yelled again.

I checked to see that the girl was gone—she was—and I ran after my brother, panting in the stench, strangely used to it. We ran and ran, down one tunnel then turned sharply into another. All of them somehow joined up, flowing together.

As we slowed to a walk, we could hear the pipes whooshing, trickling, and flushing, all the garbage from above emptying down. It was like the march of water—water musicians, water clowns, water acrobats, water slaves, water killers, the childhood of water and the death of it.

But there were no Russians there, no mother, no father, no Paul. We walked for hours. I was not hungry, only thirsty, but I would not have trusted any kind of drink available in this underground world.

We came to a wall with a hole in it barely big enough for each of us to crawl through.

"Let's go," my brother said. He looked more tired than I was. "I'll help you through first."

It was even darker in this new chamber, and the water was quieter. As I helped my brother crawl through, my flashlight was aimed high at a sign: AVENUE DU COLONEL HENRI ROL-TANGUY.

"Are we on a street?" I asked.

"*Below* the street," my brother said. "Everything here is below everything else. Look behind you."

I beamed my flashlight onto the walls around us and beyond us, down this new corridor, then dropped the light. I screamed like a girl.

"The Catacombs," my brother said. He slapped his helmet with his hand. "It's an ossuary. I read about these." I picked up the light again. My brother told me they were bones. The bones of the dead. Millions of dead. Moved here over the centuries from overloaded cemeteries. But also the dead of wars and street riots—the riots in the Place de Grève, he told me, and the rue Meslée. Many who fell during the French Revolution. People who died of the Black Death. And just people. Dead people. Dead French people.

I gazed at the rows of bones. The wall of them went on far into the darkness. The bones had been arranged in a decorative way. On the top and bottom were arm bones and leg bones, laid out neatly in rows, like bone bricks. But above, below, and in the middle were the skulls, facing out in their own rows, as if they were watchmen.

We followed a swath of red paint that rolled over a group of bones, but the bones nearest my brother had a heart painted over their surfaces, with an *L* and a *G* in the middle of the heart. L and G had come down here among the dead to be in love. I wondered if they had remembered that these bones were once other people, with flesh on their bones and eyes in their sockets, people who might also have been in love.

To the right of the heart, against its swollen curve, an

223

extra-small skull looked back at my brother and me. I thought of the little girl in the sewers. I took a step closer. I wanted to touch the small face, but it was not a face, only the bone behind it. I thought I might be taking a liberty, so I decided not to.

"Attila, let's go. Mom and Dad aren't in the Catacombs. No one is here right now."

We climbed back out through the hole to the sewers. Their odors reminded us of their force.

"Can we go home?" I said.

"Not just yet. We can't give up just yet. It's a big network of sewers, and we have to keep looking, just for a while longer." He put his hand on my shoulder, and I went with him to the left, where the sewers continued.

I didn't know if I believed Attila that our parents were in this place and that we would find them, free them, and beat a path back aboveground. But I felt I had no choice. I didn't know how far we were going or where, underneath Europe, we were heading. I would not have found my way back alone, even on the streets above, and would not have known how to ask.

The deeper in we wandered, the less I believed we would ever come up for air, and I don't think Attila thought about it or even cared. He said we could stop again. He wanted to sit down on some stone steps leading up to a black steel door, but I stayed on my feet. From the building above us, water flushed into Poo River. Attila was holding his head again, rubbing the place near the bandage. I wished he would take off the helmet.

224

And then the sound of voices echoed. They were coming this way.

My brother said they might be Russians. "Finally," he said. He got to his feet and took out his gun, but the voices sounded French. I was filled with a deep and sudden dread.

Four boys, young men, French men—why wouldn't they be French men?—turned a corner and walked right up to us as if they'd expected us to be there waiting for them. Two of them wore leather jackets. One of them was smiling. He lit a smoke with a lighter, and the flame flared wildly. I wondered if the sewers were flammable.

A tall, thin man, one of two not wearing a leather jacket, slapped my brother on the helmet from behind and chuckled. He was slightly walleyed and appeared to be staring down Attila and me at the same time. He pointed to the swastika, and then he and the other one not wearing a leather jacket each thrust an arm straight out above them. They chanted, *"Sieg heil! Sieg heil! Sieg heil!"* and goose-stepped in a circle around my brother and me. The smoker released quite a cloud of smoke and then flicked his cigarette into the river. He joined the goose-steppers, and together the four of them circled Attila and me. Attila stood, trying to shield me from harm. I clutched the flashlight in my pocket. My brother raised his gun to the smoker's face but took a terrible shove to the back, from somewhere above my head, and fell over. He sprang to his feet, and someone slapped him and said something to us in French.

The only French words I knew were the words to

"Habanera," the song from *Carmen,* which I had sung to the Gypsy on the street in Budapest. I tried out a phrase weakly: *"L'amour."* For my efforts I took a sharp slap. *"L'amour! L'amour! L'amour! L'amour!"* I said, chirping like a bird.

A cloth-coated French boy—not the walleyed one— kicked me to shut me up, and I fell to one knee. My brother rushed to my side, then went mad and sprang with his gun at the smoking boy. He ground the muzzle into the boy's cheek and screamed Hungarian swear words at him. Two of the thugs jumped back, but the one behind Attila walloped him again, and my brother pitched forward. The gun flew from his hand and cascaded along the stone floor. Attila started coughing, and when I went to embrace him, the last sound I heard was a wet thud at the back of my head.

SEVENTEEN

I SANK SOMEWHERE, possibly down into the earth. I could taste grains of earth in my mouth, like poppy seeds, but then grains of light mixed in, and grains of sound. A woman's voice. My name. I heard my name.

It was my grandmother. "Robert. Oh, my Robert."

I opened my eyes and looked around me. I was in my brother's bed in Aunt Hermina's library, with a wet cloth on my forehead. This was the bed for head-injury cases, I guess. My own bed was empty. "Where's Attila?" I asked.

My grandmother's face was grim, anxious. "My dear—you were brought back here by a guard in the city sewers. What on earth were you doing there?"

"We were trying to rescue Mom and Dad. But where's Attila?"

My grandmother hesitated. "We don't know," she said. "We were hoping you could tell us when you woke up."

"Attila wasn't with me?"

"You were alone when the guard found you," my grandmother said and took my hand. "Your parents are looking for your brother with Hermina. They're down at the police station again."

I tried to sit up, but my grandmother wouldn't let me.

"Yes, your parents are all right, dear. They're fine. A little shaken up, but they've been released. We were afraid we'd be sent back, but they couldn't tell the Russians anything they wanted to hear. They were very lucky. If we can find Attila, we'll all be very lucky."

I pictured my brother still lying down there in the sewers or dragged off somewhere by the thugs. I kept seeing that stupid helmet. Maybe the boys had yanked it off his head, kicked it around like a ball, kicked him again while he was down. Maybe he was walking the streets confused, not knowing who he was.

Anything was possible. The idea blew up in my head. I gasped. I could barely catch my breath.

Babette looked in on us then. She smiled broadly at me. I imagined she was glad to see me awake at last. She came over to stroke my cheek. I could see the love bite on her neck, the Mark of Attila.

Over the following days, my parents and the kind Hungarian doctor were often with the police, down in the sewers, searching underneath Paris. My parents had gotten off lightly, as it happened. My mother was unharmed, and while my father had a black eye and a fat lip, both of them had come back alive.

In bits of conversation between them and my grandmother and Aunt Hermina, I found out that my father
did know something about Paul—a secret that he and
Hermina had shared but hadn't let on. There was a man
they were calling a double agent, a Hungarian, who'd
acted both for the Hungarians and for the Russians. Paul
had been in the room in the Swedish embassy when this
man warned Wallenberg not to meet with the Russians.
He said they would take the Swede away, and they did.
Then a few years later, after no one had seen Paul since
he disappeared, he showed up out of nowhere in Paris
at Hermina and Ede's town house and stayed for a few
days. Hermina said it was so he could meet with this same
agent and try to find out about Wallenberg. She got hold
of my father in Budapest to let him know, but then Paul
disappeared again. Where was this man now, and where
was Paul? And how had the Russians figured out that we
were in Paris? We didn't know the answers to these questions any more than we knew where my brother was.

My grandmother and great-aunt took me all over the
city to distract me from my distress about Attila: the Eiffel
Tower, the Champs-Élysées, out to Versailles, the Notre
Dame Cathedral, with its fierce gargoyles, and café after café—Le Petit Château d'Eau, Les Deux Magots,
over on Place Saint-Germain-des-Prés, and the Café de
la Paix. I could have as much cake as I wanted as often
as I wanted, and I did. I began to learn the names of the
ones I decided I'd ask for again: éclairs, Jésuites, made
with frangipane, madeleines, gâteaux Saint-Honoré, and
a very favorite, bugnes, angel wings, ribbons of pastry

sprinkled with sugar. In each place, I hoped to find a monkey, but not a single café thought to employ one.

I fell in love with the *Venus de Milo* every bit as much as I had with the girl in the sewers and the girl with the lips at the convent, maybe more. Even as much as Babette, though possibly not Babette. I visited Venus three times. She stood there, in her lighted hall in the Louvre, and I loved the armlessness of her, the softness of her stone skin, the mad folds of her dress. She gave you the impression that a sculptor had begun a shape for her and then given her over to the wind and the rain and the moon to finish her, over time, over many years, but never aging her, never daring to. I wanted badly to bundle her up with me, offer her a pair of the long wooden hands of my great-aunt, and steal her far away.

And each day when we got home, I raced in, hoping to find my brother. Each day, he was not there.

One evening over dinner I said to my family, "I couldn't stop him." No one answered, so I said it again. "I couldn't stop Attila."

"Why not?" my father asked.

"Simon!" my mother said.

"Why couldn't he?" he said. He set down his fork.

"Could you have stopped him?" my grandmother asked him. "Can I stop *you?* Can you stop yourself, once you get started?"

My father got to his feet, squeezed my shoulder, and walked out.

Aunt Hermina invited me into the solarium to hear something. "It's my favorite show in English," she said.

"It's from America. Come, let's catch a bit of it." She turned on the great wooden radio console and fidgeted with it to find the station. She even had to pull off a glove to get it right.

A strange voice came on. He was singing.

"It's Jimmy Durante," she told me. "Listen."

Jimmy was singing a sad song, but his voice was raspy, as if the dial weren't quite set on it. I wanted to give him a candy for his throat, but his voice was as warm as could be. I wondered what my grandfather Robert's voice had been like, whether it was raspy and warm too.

When Jimmy wound down, the audience roared. He said, "Good night, Mrs. Calabash, wherever you are."

"What is he saying?" I asked.

My great-aunt told me. I asked who Mrs. Calabash was, and she couldn't say. "It might not be anyone, really," she said, "or maybe she's a friend, or she's his sweetheart."

With a voice that warm, I wanted it to be his sweetheart, wherever she was.

On the seventh day word came about Attila. It came in the morning by phone. I was having breakfast, the last one to do so, eating eggs again, poking the dark lace at the edge with my fork the way Attila always did.

My brother had been found. He had washed up in the sewers somewhere, hardly identifiable, covered in sludge but still wearing his helmet.

EIGHTEEN

ATTILA WAS BURIED right next to our uncle Ede in Père Lachaise Cemetery, over in the 20th arrondissement. The cemetery was an untidy gallery of sculptures, some of them angels, a single dog, some human figures, and some parts of humans—mostly hands and heads, praying hands or questioning heads and sad heads. They waited patiently for the wind and rain to take them away. But it was sunny on this day, and what wind there was whistled to the stones and visitors. My mother had lost her voice and her smile. She looked like someone sleepwalking. My grandmother took her by the hand and led her away from the grave.

I remembered the Catacombs. I looked back over my shoulder to where we'd laid my brother, and I shuddered. Was it possible that we were just going to leave him there?

My ears were ringing. I didn't want my brother to have a headstone. I wanted him to have a monument worthy of the Statue Graveyard. But his statue wouldn't wear a helmet like the one he had on in the sewers. Instead I'd have him sit in his own chair beside Mor Jokai at the head of our street back home.

My father took my mother in his arms, and they swayed to and fro. They didn't want to look back at my brother.

My great-aunt said quietly to my grandmother, "Sometimes I feel more left behind than living." Mamu looked at her sister as if to answer, but she didn't.

I hoped the going down of my brother was like everything else he did, just a switch—switch on, switch off. Sudden, not gradual.

A bird zinged past us and landed on a nearby branch, where it began to sing like mad. What came first—music or birds? A question Attila might have asked. Did music live in the mind of the Lord up until the day he wrapped feathers and wings around it?

Finally, we trudged out of Père Lachaise Cemetery, hanging on to pieces of each other. We must have looked scary, like a family damned, a family trying out for horror pictures.

After that, Attila cast a blue light over everything. Every sight, every thought was tinged with it. And not the blue light of the sky but the blue of lanes and back alleys, where people meet in secret or pass through quickly on their way to better light. Sometimes the blue made a sound, a humming, and sometimes a soft ringing, which I tried to interpret just before it faded.

I developed a rash. Often in this strange light I watched the blue flakes flying off me and studied them, considering whether any might be Attila, if I was what was left of the world. What would it feel like to die off and take flight, believing that a new cell would take your place, or not knowing for sure, not knowing anything for sure anymore?

I picked at the blue flakes and asked them where they were going. Food for mites. Blue mite shit left behind to grow more things, upward toward the brighter blue sky.

NINETEEN

IT KILLED ME THAT Attila never got to think and speak in English the way I can now. It was the strangest thing at first, like having a foreign invader living inside your head. If he could have, I know my brother would have asked his questions in English with the same force as always. He would be the cowboy rabbi. And he would have been the first to lead a search party for Mrs. Calabash.

Mrs. Calabash was somewhere, if somewhere was anywhere. Somewhere was where Paul was. I wondered if we would ever find him, this man who had saved my family. Where would we begin to look and when? And would it matter?

A week after we buried my brother, we boarded a ship called the *Jean-Jacques Rousseau* in Nantes, an old slaving port, my grandmother told me. She held my mother's hand quite a bit of the time. The two sat staring at a radio in our cabin, though the radio was not on. Sometimes they bobbed like someone rocking a baby. My mother had taken to not speaking to my father at all, so I was concerned about both of them. My father spent hours in the ship's bar, but thirst was not the issue, so the one-eyed drink stared up at him, neglected, the whole day through.

I heard my grandmother whisper to my mother in the dark one night that Attila's death was senseless, like the deaths of my mother's parents and brothers and sisters in the Hitler war. But what death was sensible? In my 9.8 years on earth, almost 9.9, I had not yet encountered a death that made sense. It was hard to understand what Adam and Eve had set in motion. Even they must have had trouble understanding once Cain and Abel went at each other.

Now and again, I picture my golden brother lying there in that box in the ground at Père Lachaise, the worms nibbling away at his thoughts and questions, and not even silkworms.

I'd added my brother to my Afterlife Portfolio, elevated him to the head of it, above the sheep and the dead men and Judit, not to mention Medea's children, Mermeros and Pheres, as well as Castor and Pollux, the Brothers Goose, the Brothers Grimm, the Brothers Karamazov, and even the stars.

Attila and I didn't mean for the fish to take wing or the stars to tell us old stories. We didn't want to offend anyone. We meant only to ask questions.

When we were boarding the ship, my parents let me

take my brother's satchel along with my own. A porter helped with our new suitcases, and my father carried both of the satchels for me. He also carried a cloth bag holding the two Mark Twain books together in their leather case. It wasn't until we were in our cabin that I opened my brother's bag for the first time. In it, he had several items, including his Scarecrow Pez, the letters to Hermina from Mamu, the *Schutz-Passes,* and his cowboy gun, belt, and spurs, of course, plus a hunting knife. But I was surprised to find that he had also stashed away my crayon drawing of the sunflowers, the one I thought I'd lost.

Maybe my brother had been wrong about the sun. Maybe the sun's aim was to set fire to the sky, but it wasn't strong enough. It was very strong, but not strong enough to do that. The sun could have been a fluttering thing just as easily as a ball, fanning out waves of light and gusts of warmth. I kept taking out my brother's picture of the Spitfire and the sun firing out rays in the same way, and holding it next to my drawing of the sunflowers.

The very first night at sea, my father asked if I wanted to get some air. He still had his black eye, but it was fading to purple and violet now, like smeared makeup. We stood out on deck together. At last he was going to say something, I could tell, and I wondered what I'd answer. But there was that blue film again—we were both looking through it—and he didn't say a thing. He just took hold of the back of my neck, put a soft clamp on it, and then walked away, leaving me alone.

I turned back to the ocean, and for a second I thought I'd seen a shape out on the water. I couldn't make out what it was or who it was. I wanted to call out to it, but then the shape folded itself into the dark water again.

I wondered where my brother was at the moment. I didn't really believe he was in Père Lachaise Cemetery. Had he stopped off on the moon for a break from his long journey? But there was hardly any moon that night. It was black out, a deep black, as black up and down and ahead and behind us as it must have been the day God had decided to switch on the light. I thought of all that unmade light, all the unmade eyes waiting to receive it, and wondered where the Lord must have bundled it.

But even the black was tinged with blue, and in this bluing over of things, I thought again that I spotted something out on the water. I was certain it was my brother, a good-size tail glinting up behind him. He was a blue merman except with golden hair, even in this light. I felt a rush—was he waving to me? Mouthing something? I was desperate to answer. I called out his name like mad. He mouthed something else, but I could not read his lips. Still I felt strangely uplifted.

I don't know what's next after humans. I was hoping Attila could ask the Powers That Be and send me a signal.

There was a cooing behind me. When I turned, a young woman was sitting on a bench under the glow of a deck light, feeding her nipple to her excited infant, who could have passed, with its black fuzzy hair, for a monkey. When the little thing had latched on finally, the woman babbled joyously at her baby, and I thought, at first, she must have been Hungarian. But it was only the sounds that were familiar, not the words.

Her baby was as content as could be—and what a clever size it was! You've got to wonder: What came first—the design of the womb or the size of the baby? Should it be just big enough to take up shelter inside its mother? What an interesting challenge it must have been for the Lord. Should I make the baby small, the size of a guppy, make a thousand of them at a time? Should I make it bigger but still small enough to grow inside an egg until it can break free? How about a full-size new-born—have it grow until it's as big as its mother, turning her inside out to break free? Or how about unfurling it from her mouth, like a magician's mouth, like a long rib-bon remaking itself before her eyes?

After realizing that the young mother was not Hun-garian, I'd given up hope of seeing anyone I knew when, walking on deck the next evening, I ran into the tall boy who'd been on the rival swim team from Saint Hilda's School in Budapest, the boy whose name my brother had forgotten and who had forgotten my brother's name. It turned out the boy's name was Sandor. I wished I could tell Attila.

"Where's your brother?" the boy asked me.

"He didn't make it," I said. I told him the story, and Sandor shrugged, looked down a distance at his feet, then asked if I wanted to see something. "Sure," I said.

He took me to his cabin and pulled out a radio from under his bed. "It's a shortwave," he said. He plugged it in and fiddled quite a bit with it and then said, "Listen."

There was static, but a man's voice, a radio announcer, broke through the crackle.

"What is it?" I asked.

"It's a radio station from Canada," Sandor said. "Ontario. He's saying the weather."

"How do you know?"

"I know some English. My mother is English."

"What's the man saying?" I asked.

"The man is saying snow—there's a lot of snow falling. It's a weather forecast, and he's naming the Ontario counties and towns. An early blast of winter—in November!"

"Snow," I repeated, my new English word.

We listened. The radio man's voice sounded soft and calm. I did not know the names then, but I have heard them many times since, lying alone in my room, listening to the feathery snow tick against the window as I wait for sleep: *Essex, Kent, Lambton, Elgin, Middlesex: snow, high of twelve. Huron, Perth, Grey, Bruce, Waterloo, Wellington, Oxford, Brant: snow, heavy at times, high of eight. York, Durham, Belleville, Quinte, Northumberland: snow, mixed with freezing rain. Peterborough and the Kawarthas, Parry Sound, Muskoka: heavy snow, whiteout conditions through the night, and bitterly cold, high of minus twenty-two. Algonquin, Renfrew, Pembroke, Barry's Bay: periods of snow, clearing in the morning, high of eight. Ottawa, Prescott, Russell, Cornwall, Morrisburg: light snow, but very cold, high of minus seven. Wawa, the Sault, Cochrane, Timmins, Lake of the Woods: whiteout conditions, high of minus twenty.*

It sounded as if the gentle radio announcer were calling each of his children to bed, by name, one by one.

I went back out on deck after that to watch the great

beast of a ship sloshing along, clearing a path through all those fluttering, quivering, and slithering things in the deep waters below us, a path through all that striving. The sky was a clear black but flecked with stars, like notes flung over the hood of the Atlantic, glowheads each and every one. I swear I could hear them twinkle. *Twinkle* is too childish a word, but look at them. How else can you say it? It's what they want you to say.

ACKNOWLEDGMENTS

I am deeply grateful to Byrd Leavell and Julie Stevenson for taking a chance on me, and to Mike Sacks for recommending me to Byrd. I thank my editor at Little, Brown, the inimitable Ben George. What hours and love he put into this novel! I also thank Ben Allen, Ashley Marudas, Tracy Williams, Sarah Haugen, as well as the many other good people at Little, Brown.

I thank the people who gave me advice on earlier versions of the manuscript: foremost among them Ken Ballen, but also Richard Bausch, Barbara Berson, David Bezmozgis, Andrew Clark, Trevor Cole, Margaret Hart, Peter Kertes, and Antanas Sileika. I thank two eternal fans: Athena Papageorge and Vassiliki Daskalaki.

I thank my dear Helen, Angela, Natalie, Peter, Jordan, Rob, and now Dylan, who have cheered me on all these years.